"WHAT'S DOG MAGIC?" KATE ASKED.

"Dog Magic," Toby told Kate and Matt, "is just the special magic we dogs have. You know, our little ways of doing things, like finding our way home even if the scent's been covered over, or knowing when Matt is on his way home from school, even before I can hear him."

"Oh," commented Kate. "That doesn't sound like magic."

"Well," Toby explained, "it is. It's dog magic. All of us animals have magic, each our own kind. But to *talk*, well, that takes a special kind of dog magic. For that a dog must be very desperate and very lucky, too. Every night Polly and I prayed to Sirius that I would be granted human speech so I could get you and Matt to help me."

"Sirius?" Kate asked. "Who's that?"

Toby looked suprised. "Why, Sirius is the Dog Star," he said.

"The brightest star in the heavens, and the guardian of canines."

Can Sirius—and dog magic—help Matt and Kate find Toby's puppies?

DOG MAGIC

Anna Coates

A BANTAM SKYLARK BOOK ®
NEW YORK · TORONTO · LONDON · SYDNEY · AUCKLAND

RL 4, 008–012

DOG MAGIC

A Bantam Skylark Book / December 1991

*Skylark Books is a registered trademark of Bantam Books,
a division of Bantam Doubleday Dell Publishing Group, Inc.
Registered in U.S. Patent and Trademark Office and elsewhere.*

ISBN 0-553-15910-0

Published simultaneously in the United States and Canada

*Bantam Books are published by Bantam Books, a division of Bantam
Doubleday Dell Publishing Group, Inc. Its trademark, consisting of
the words "Bantam Books" and the portrayal of a rooster, is Reg-
istered in U.S. Patent and Trademark Office and in other countries.
Marca Registrada. Bantam Books, 666 Fifth Avenue, New York, New
York 10103.*

PRINTED IN THE UNITED STATES OF AMERICA

CWO 0 9 8 7 6 5 4 3 2 1

For the real Matthew

Chapter One

There was not even a hint of magic in the air that Thursday afternoon in late summer. Matthew and Kate Baker had no idea that what was about to happen would change their lives.

The Los Angeles smog was thick and heavy, and Matthew and Kate had decided to stay indoors. Matt's mother called this part of August the "dog days," but Matt didn't see why. His dog, Toby, didn't seem to like the heat any more than he did.

Matthew's little sister, Kate, lay on her stomach with her arm slung over Toby. She was watching an *I Love Lucy* rerun on television.

1

att sighed and wished his mother were home he could drive them over to the public pool. It was awfully hot. He could have walked to the pool himself, but Kate wasn't allowed to swim unless their mother was there, and Matthew wasn't allowed to leave her alone at the house for more than thirty minutes. Kate was eight, but sometimes she acted like a big baby. She wasn't allowed to do all the things Matthew had been able to do when he was eight, three years before.

Their mother had wanted to enroll Kate in day camp for the summer, but Kate had begged to be allowed to stay home, and Matthew had promised to watch her and to take care of her, every day, all summer long.

"Stop it, Toby," Kate said. Toby licked her face again, and she sat up, frowning. "Matthew, make him *stop*."

"Here, boy," Matt called. Toby got up and padded over to him. Toby was a medium-size dog, not quite as big as an Irish setter, but bigger than a cocker spaniel. He had long, silky fur like a setter's, and it was the soft tan color of a spaniel's coat. His body was lean, and he had big, friendly brown eyes and a golden plume of a tail that always seemed to be wagging.

Toby whined and Matthew scratched under his chin. "What's the matter, boy? Want to go for a walk?"

Toby's ears perked up, but then they drooped again. He sat down by Matthew's feet, and then he got up again and rested his chin on Matthew's knee.

"I know, boy," Matt said, stroking Toby's soft fur. "It's hot, isn't it. And you're wearing a fur coat, too. Poor boy."

Toby shook Matt's hand off and looked up at him. His eyes seemed worried and sad. Then the amazing thing happened.

"Master," Toby said softly. "Please help me."

Matthew stared at the dog in astonishment. "I," he said. "You, I mean. *What?*"

Kate sat up and laughed. "That sounded so *real*, Matt," she said.

"But," Matthew protested, "that wasn't me. That was *Toby.*"

Kate laughed again and went into the kitchen.

Matthew looked at the dog out of the corner of his eye. "Toby," he whispered. "Did you say something?"

Toby whined and thumped his tail against the floor. He seemed so friendly and back to normal that Matthew decided his mind must be playing tricks on him.

"Yes, Master," Toby said. "I said, please help me."

Matthew's heart was pounding as he looked around the room. He could hear Kate in the kitchen, so he knew it couldn't be *her* playing a trick on *him*. Besides, Kate would never be able to keep from laughing for so long. And he'd heard the words come right out of Toby's mouth.

Matthew was not very good in school, but he had plenty of common sense. It came to his rescue now.

"Toby," he said softly, "what's the matter?"

Toby stood up and wagged his tail enthusiastically. "I knew it," he said happily. "I knew I could speak human language, if I just tried hard enough and prayed for dog magic. Polly didn't think so, but I *told* her you'd understand me. I just knew you would!"

Fascinated, Matthew watched the dog. Toby's tail drooped and his eyes lost their happy expression. "That's what this is all about, Master," he said sadly. "You know Polly, the little sheltie who lives with the Brown family?"

Matthew nodded. "I see her on my way to

school sometimes, in their yard. She always barks at me."

Toby hung his head. "I'm sorry she barks, Master. She doesn't mean any harm. It's just that she knows I live with you, and she wishes you'd come over and say hello."

"I might if she didn't act so ferocious!" Matthew said.

"Oh, Master!" Toby whined softly under his breath. "Polly would never hurt anyone, *never*. She's gentle and so sweet. And besides," he added, "Polly is a mother."

"Oh, yeah!" Matt smiled, remembering the litter of half-grown pups he'd seen tumbling in the Browns' front yard. He thought there were four of them, all of different shapes and sizes. "That's right," he went on. "The Browns were wondering how Polly got, I mean—*you know*—who the father dog was."

Toby put his head up and let his ears rise into points. "I am their father," he announced proudly. "Polly is my wife."

It seemed as though Toby were about to say something more, but just then Kate came in from the kitchen and let out a wail. "Stop it!" she yelled. Her face was as round and red as an apple.

5

"You just stop it right now, Matthew Baker! That's not funny, and you're scaring me."

"But, Kate," Matt insisted. "It's not me. Toby's really talking. And anyway, Kate, you don't have to be scared of *Toby*. He's our dog!"

Toby wagged his tail in agreement, but wisely kept silent.

"Oh, sure," Kate said suspiciously.

"No," Matt said. "Really, Kate. Listen. Toby, *speak*."

Toby looked up at Matt for a moment, puzzled. Then he sat down on his hind legs, put his front paws in the air, and barked twice.

Matt frowned. He had taught Toby that trick when he was just a tiny pup. "No, boy," he said. "I meant, say something in English. Please."

Toby looked a little hurt, but he put his front paws down and licked his chops. "I don't want to scare her," he said softly.

"Aaaaah!" yelled Kate. "I told you, *stop* it, Matthew!" She screwed her face up as if she were about to cry, and then she ran out of the living room. Matt heard the door to their mother's bedroom slam shut. Kate had to share a room with their mother, but she had a separate bed of her own with curtains around it on three sides and a little desk and bookshelf on the other. When she

6

felt angry or sad, she would climb into her bed and pull the curtains shut. No one, not Matthew or their mother, was supposed to bother her until she decided to come out.

Matthew looked at Toby and shrugged. "Don't worry, Tobe. She'll get bored and come out. Finish telling me about Polly and the puppies and everything."

"Well, Master," Toby began, but Matt interrupted.

"Toby," he said uncomfortably. "Why do you keep calling me Master? Can't you just call me Matt, like everybody else does?"

Toby's brown eyes widened. "Everybody calls you Master," he replied. "At least, when they're talking to me, they do. Kate says, 'Toby, take this to your master,' when she gives me the ball to play with, and Mom says, 'Toby, tell your master it's time for your supper, and—"

"Mom!" Matt exclaimed, laughing again. "Do you mean *my* mom, mine and Kate's?"

Toby sighed and lowered his head. Matt realized he had embarrassed the dog, and he stopped laughing. "I'm sorry," he said. "It just sounded funny, that's all. Her name is Gretchen, or Mrs. Baker. Mom is just what we call her."

"I know that," Toby said. "But I sort of think

7

of her as Mom, too. I mean, I don't even re-member my real mother. Her name was Wanda Lee Beauty, but I left her when I was just weaned.''

"I'm sorry," Matt said again. He scratched be-hind Toby's ears, and the dog seemed to cheer up. "So what is it you need help with, Tobe? Is it something about Polly and the pups?"

The dog wagged his tail. "Mr. Brown told Polly the pups were going to good homes," he said. "He put an ad in the newspaper, and a very nice lady came to the house last weekend. She said she would take all the puppies and send them to live on a nice farm where there'd be lots of room to run, and children to play with, and plenty of good food to eat."

Toby's voice dropped nearly to a whisper as he went on. "And, Master—I mean, *Matt*. She said she wanted the littlest pup, our Ranger, for her own dog."

"I'm sorry, Toby," Matt said. He had never thought of how hard it must be for a mother and father dog to give up their litter. It would be like his mother's having to give him and Kate up, he supposed. "It sounds as though your puppies have good homes, at least, but poor Polly must miss them a lot."

8

"Oh, Matt, that's not it," Toby said.

"Then," asked Matthew, "what's the problem?"

"Oh, Matt, it's awful!" To Matthew's amazement, Toby got up and slunk over to the big stereo cabinet with his tail between his legs. He was crying softly, the way he did when Matt's mother scolded him for barking or chewing shoes. He scrunched his body up and slid under the stereo cabinet and lay there with his paws over his nose.

"Toby!" Matt exclaimed. He crossed the room and got down on his knees in front of the cabinet. "Come on out, Tobe, and finish what you were telling me."

"It's too awful," Toby whined. "It's too awful."

Matt lay down on his stomach and stuck his arm under the cabinet until he touched soft fur. "Come on, pal," he said softly. "I can't help unless you tell me what's the matter."

Toby whined again, but didn't answer.

"Haven't I always taken care of you?" Matt asked.

"Well," Toby said, "you used to forget my dinner sometimes, and Mom—I mean, Gretchen—would have to make it."

"But not for years." Matt flushed. "That was when I was a baby. I'm *eleven* now, and I take good care of you."

Toby wouldn't budge.

Matthew sat up, confused. Sometimes Toby was hard to understand. Then he had an idea.

"Toby," Matt said quietly. "I feed you and let you out and keep your coat brushed. But it's really *you* who takes care of *us*, isn't it? You guard the house when we're not here, and you listen for burglars and . . . and *monsters* at night, don't you? You've always looked after me and Kate, especially since Dad died, haven't you?"

Toby growled deep and loud, from way back in his throat. "And Gretchen!" he shouted. "I look after the whole house. It's my job." He slid out from under the cabinet. "No one dares to enter this house without my permission!" he yelled. He barked twice and hopped up onto the couch, where he was not supposed to go. "I'd bite a burglar! I'd rip his clothes and sink my teeth into his leg! I'd eat a monster alive if one dared come in this house, but none does, because a mean, fierce *dog* lives here." Toby barked again, and then he jumped off the couch and raced around the room three times.

10

"That's it, boy," Matt said happily. "Now, tell me what's the matter. Is something wrong with the puppies? Are they in danger?"

Toby stopped abruptly. He went to Matt and sat down beside him on the floor. "I believe so," Toby said softly. "I don't think that nice lady took our pups to a farm at all, and I don't think she took Ranger home to live with her, either."

"But, Toby," Matt said, "what makes you think that?"

"Mrs. Mulligan's shepherd dog, Sergeant, told us," Toby said. "Mrs. Mulligan is too old to walk him a lot, so he jumps over the back fence. He goes far and wide, believe me. Sergeant was there the day the lady took the pups, and he recognized her. He says she lives not too far from here, in an apartment on Wilshire Boulevard." Toby trembled. "That's a horrible street," he said. "Full of cars, racing as fast as they can, just looking for dogs to run over."

"Go on," Matt said impatiently. "What about your puppies?"

"Well," Toby continued, "the building where this lady lives is called the Glen Wilshire Arms. It's about a thousand or two thousand floors high. Sergeant says the rule in that building is strictly *no pets allowed*. If there was a puppy on the premises, Sergeant would know it!"

Matt stared at the dog. "You mean the lady *lied*, Toby? But why? Why would anybody lie to get your puppies?"

Chapter Two

✛

"So, you see, Matt," Toby was saying, "why Polly and I are so wor—"

Toby suddenly stopped talking. His ears stood straight up, and he padded swiftly to the front door.

"What is it?" Matt started to ask, but then he heard keys jingling. A moment later his mother flung open the door. "Kids!" she called. "Matt, Kate, I'm home." Toby trotted over and rubbed against Mrs. Baker's legs. She bent down and scratched behind his ears. "Hey, boy," she said. Then she put her briefcase down by the door and leaned over to kiss Matthew. "Hi, honey."

"Mom!" Kate appeared in the hallway. Her eyes were red and swollen from crying. "Matt was teasing me," she complained. "He was pretending Toby was talking, and when I said it scared me, he wouldn't stop."

"Oh, my," Mrs. Baker said. "He was pretending Toby could talk? That must have been terrifying." A little smile danced around her mouth, and Matt had to smile, too, watching her.

"It *was*," Kate protested.

"I wasn't playing, Mom," Matt said. "Toby really was talking! Want to see for yourself?"

Matt put his hand on the top of Toby's head, and the dog wagged his tail agreeably.

"Okay, kids," Mrs. Baker said wearily. "Just let me get my shoes off and glance through the mail, and then we'll talk about it. Okay?"

She stepped out of her shoes and scooped the mail off the hall table. "Bills," she said with a sigh, looking down at the envelope on top of the stack.

Matt tugged on Toby's collar and followed his mother into the living room. "Toby," he said, "please say something to my mother."

Toby lay down on the floor and put his chin on his paws.

"Come on, Toby," Matt said, a little annoyed. "Speak up."

14

Toby whined and looked up at Matt blankly.

"Yeah, Toby," Kate said, making her voice all smart-alecky. "Say, *'Master, help me.'*"

"Kate," Mrs. Baker said, looking up from the papers on her lap. "What are you talking about?"

Kate ignored her mother and dropped onto all fours on the carpet. She narrowed her eyes and growled at Matthew. "Help me," she said again, "or I'll bite your leg." Then she grabbed Matt's leg with one hand and started tearing at his jeans with her teeth. "Grrrr," she said. "Grrrr."

"Kate," Mrs. Baker said sharply. "Get *up*!"

"Yeah," Matt said angrily, yanking his leg away from her. "Get up and shut up!"

"Matthew." Mrs. Baker stood up and looked down at the children. "You will not speak to your sister in that fashion. Do you understand me?"

"Yes, Mom," Matt said meekly. He stared at Toby, wishing the dog would say something and get him out of this mess.

"Kate," Mrs. Baker went on, "get up and apologize to your brother. Then wash your hands and set the table. Please."

"All right," Kate said sullenly. "Sorry," she muttered at Matthew.

"Sorry, *what*?" Mrs. Baker asked. It was a rule at their house, when you apologized to someone

15

you had to say the person's name, too, to show you meant it.

Kate couldn't resist. "Sorry, *Master*," she said, laughing. Matthew jumped up and grabbed for her, but she twisted away and stuck out her tongue at him.

Matthew looked down at Toby, furious. "Why don't you say something?" he shouted. "Cat got your tongue?"

Toby stood up and stretched. "There's no reason to be insulting," he said mildly. "I didn't say anything because it wouldn't do any good."

"Not do any good? Hah!" Matthew smiled triumphantly. Kate was staring at the dog, her mouth opened into a surprised "O."

"Toby," Mrs. Baker said, sounding very irritated. "Stop that barking!"

"Told you so," Toby said, lying down again. "She can't understand a word I'm saying."

"But, Mom," Matthew argued. He wanted to explain that what sounded to her like ordinary barking was plain English to him and Kate. "See, we—"

"Matt," Toby said. "She can't—"

"Toby!" Mrs. Baker shook her finger and spoke sharply. "I said hush!"

"Toby?" Kate asked. "You did talk, didn't you?

16

You did!'' A wide, happy smile broke across her face, but that didn't make Matt feel any better.

"Kate, don't you start, too,'' Mrs. Baker warned, pressing the cool palm of her hand across Matthew's face. "I believe your forehead is a little warm,'' she said. "I want you to take a nap before dinner, honey.''

Matt tried again to explain. But another sharp look from his mother sent him straight to his room. He was too excited to sleep, so instead he got out his drawing tablet and sketched some action figures from memory.

Sometimes Matthew wished drawing were one of the important subjects in school, like math and English and social studies. He was better at drawing than at anything else, although his mother couldn't understand why. "Matt,'' she'd say, looking at his report card, "I don't understand it. You read everything from encyclopedias to soup can labels. How can you get a D in English? And a C in math? Your father had a degree in accounting, for goodness' sake! You have to have gotten some of his talent.''

Matt didn't think he'd gotten much of his father's talent, or his mother's, either. Kate had gotten everything. She was only going into the third grade, but you could already tell she was going to be good in school. She was pretty, too. At least, Matthew thought she was, when she wasn't crying or yelling her head off about something.

Matt sighed and put his tablet down. The next thing he knew, someone was shaking him.

"Matthew," Kate whispered, shaking him again. "Wake up. It's time for dinner."

Matt stared at her, trying to remember why he had the strange, shaky feeling he always got when something special was about to happen.

"I'm sorry I didn't believe you," Kate said, folding her hands in front of her. Then she put her hands on her hips and scowled. "But it's your fault, for always trying to scare me."

"It's okay," Matt said, sitting up.

"And I'm sorry I was scared of Toby," Kate added. "I already told him."

"It's okay," Matt said again. "Where is he? Did he say anything else?"

Kate shook her head. "He's sleeping in the hall. I waited till Mom started cooking, and then I whispered to him not to say anything else until he could be alone with you and me. I don't think," she added, "that Mom wants to hear us talking to him anymore."

Matt nodded. "I know, we're *getting on her nerves*," he said. The way he said it sounded ex-

18

actly like their mother, and they both burst out laughing. "What's for dinner?"

"Liver," Kate teased. "And cauliflower with gross yellow sauce, and beets."

But Matt could already smell cheese enchiladas and corn on the cob. His mouth watered as he and Kate went into the dining room to eat.

After dinner Matthew suggested that their mother go into the living room and relax while he and Kate did the dishes. Mrs. Baker looked at them a little suspiciously, but she shrugged and set down the plate she'd begun to scrape.

"Thanks for volunteering me," Kate grumbled when their mother had gone into the other room.

Toby came out from under the table. "Well," he asked Matt, "have you thought it over? Will you help me find out what's happened to the puppies?"

Matt nodded. "Of course," he answered. He quickly filled Kate in on everything Toby had told him.

"But, Matt," Kate replied, "how are you going to find out what happened to them?"

"Well," he said simply, "I'm going to go over and ask Mr. and Mrs. Brown. In fact, we'll all go."

"Good idea," Toby agreed. "Polly says they are

19

lovely people. I'll bet Sarge is all confused. The lady who lives in the no-pets building probably isn't the same one who took the dogs at all.''

Toby's words were cheerful, but Matt noticed a thick wrinkle in the golden fur between his eyes. ''Try not to worry about it too much, Tobe,'' Matt said, stroking the dog's silky coat. ''We can't go out tonight. Mom wouldn't let us. But we'll go first thing in the morning.''

''Tobe,'' Kate interrupted. ''How come Mom can't understand you? I think you talk *great*. And you're smart, too, for a dog. At least as smart as someone in kindergarten.''

Toby wagged his tail. ''My speech is clear to you,'' he said modestly. ''But I was pretty sure an adult wouldn't be able to understand me. Polly was right about that much.''

Seeing that the children didn't understand, he tried to explain. ''It's not just a matter of *understanding* your language,'' he said. ''Human talk is pretty easy to understand, since we dogs grow up with people all around us. But speaking it, that's a different matter. Some of the old hounds say there was a time when all of the animals could understand each other—humans and dogs and birds and guinea pigs. And even cats.''

Toby lowered his ears and licked his chops. ''Although I doubt you'd find a cat going out of its way to understand anybody but another cat,'' he added contemptuously.

''What happened?'' Kate broke in. ''How come we can't all understand each other anymore?''

''Well,'' Toby said, ''we do, a little bit. Dogs understand humans, and sometimes humans understand dogs, too. Mom always knows when I don't feel well, or when I want my dinner, or if I need to go outside.''

''Mom?'' Kate started to laugh, but Matthew shot her a warning look.

''*Gretchen*, I mean,'' Toby said. ''Your dear mother. But somehow, over time, you humans have come to understand less and less of what the rest of us animals are saying. And I must confess, it's not only humans who've lost the talent. Half the time I can't understand what the birds in our own backyard are chattering about, myself. But I knew dog magic would be strong enough to make *us* understand each other. Adults, well, they're a different story. I was pretty sure it wouldn't work with them. They're a little harder to communicate with, anyway. It's not that they don't have the ability to understand. Of course they do, especially the nice ones, like Gretchen. It's more just that,

21

well, they don't *know* they have the ability. You know what I mean?''

''No,'' said Matthew.

''Yes,'' said Kate.

Matt looked at her in surprise.

''Grown-ups don't believe in things they don't understand,'' she told him. ''If grown-ups can't explain something, then they don't think it's true. And since dogs aren't supposed to talk, well, then grown-ups can't hear it when they do. Right, Toby?''

Toby looked uncomfortable. ''Well,'' he said at last, ''I suppose that's it. But it's not as if they're all the same. Why, Gretchen's a grown-up, and she's just *lovely*.''

The door to the dining room flew open, and Mrs. Baker stuck her head in. ''What on earth are you doing to poor Toby?'' she asked. ''Why is he growling and woofing that way? Are you teasing him, Matthew?''

Matt hastily got up from the table and picked up an armload of dirty dishes. ''No, Mom,'' he said. ''We're just playing.''

''Well, for goodness' sake, keep it down. And give Toby those leftover scraps,'' she added, closing the door again.

Matt carried the dishes into the kitchen, and

when he came back, he had the last enchilada on a paper towel.

"But, Toby," Kate said. "What's *dog magic*?"

"Excuse me," Toby told her, looking up at Matt. He sniffed hungrily. "Is that for me?"

Matt smiled. "Of course. Here you go." He put the paper towel on the ground, and Toby snatched the enchilada off it. Then he looked at the children, a little embarrassed. "Excuse me," he said again. "I'll just tuck this away for later."

The children watched as he carried the food into the kitchen. They heard it plop into his dish, and a moment later he returned.

"Dog magic," Toby explained to Kate, "is just the special magic we dogs have. You know, our little ways of doing things, like finding our way home even if the scent's been covered over, or . . . or knowing when the master—I mean, when *Matt*—is on his way home from school, even before I can hear him. You know."

"Oh," commented Kate. "That doesn't sound like magic."

"Well," Toby replied, "it is. It's dog magic. All of us animals have magic, each our own kind."

"But," Kate protested, "people are animals, too. My teacher said so, and Mom says she's right. So why don't we have magic of our own?

"But," Toby exclaimed in surprise, "of course you do! I mean, not that silly hocus-pocus stuff, spells and tricks and things I've seen on television. You humans have radios and television, and that thing you talk into—I know, the telephone! And you've got matches, you can make *fires*, and build things, and open up cans of good things to eat." Toby licked his chops hungrily. Matthew wondered if he was thinking about the enchilada in the kitchen.

"Oh," Kate sounded disappointed. "That stuff isn't magic. It's, you know—"

"Science," Matt interjected, and Kate nodded.

"Yeah, *science*."

"Well," Toby said. "It seems like magic to me. What's the difference, anyway, what you call it? To me it's as much magic as for a bird to know north from south, and when it's time to build a nest, and where to dig for worms.

"But to *talk*," Toby went on, "well, that takes a special kind of dog magic. For that a dog must be very desperate—and very lucky, too. Every night Polly and I prayed to Sirius that I would be granted human speech so I could get you and Matt to help me."

"Sirius?" Kate asked. "Who's that?"

Toby looked surprised. "Why, Sirius is the Dog

24

Star," he said. "The brightest star in the heavens, and the guardian of canines. Dogs, that is. Some of the pups say it's just doglore, but the old hounds say, 'If you need a miracle, and all else fails, pray to Sirius, and he will answer.' "

Toby whined and slipped his nose under Kate's palm. She scratched behind his ears and under his collar.

"Well," Matthew said at last. "Come on, Kate. Let's finish the dishes and go to bed. We'll get up early tomorrow and go over to the Browns'."

Toby sat up. "Could you let me out first?" he asked Kate. "I'd like to run over to the Browns' myself, and say good-night to Polly."

Kate walked Toby to the front hall and opened the door for him. "Careful, boy," she said. "Watch for cars."

Kate glanced into the living room, where her mother sat in the soft yellow circle of the lamp, reading a book.

"And Toby," she called softly, "tell Polly not to worry too much. We'll find those pups and make sure they're okay. I promise."

Kate wasn't sure, but she thought she heard a muffled answering bark from way down the block, where Toby had disappeared. When Kate walked through the living room, her mother looked up at her, as if she wanted to say something. But then the moment passed. Mrs. Baker bent over her book, and Kate pulled open the folding door that led to the kitchen.

Chapter Three

Matthew thought that he'd have to sneak into his mother's room to awaken Kate, but she was already in the kitchen eating cereal when he finished in the bathroom.

"No more milk," Kate said with her mouth full. It sounded like "Oo mo mih," but Matt knew what she meant. "I made you an English muffin, though."

Matt took his muffin from the toaster oven and spread a thick layer of strawberry jam over it. He put it on a folded paper towel, and then he went to the refrigerator and took out the pitcher of orange juice. There wasn't much else in there to eat, and Matt hoped their mother would stop on the way home from work and pick up something good. Sometimes she'd give Matt ten dollars and let him walk over to the fried chicken restaurant or to the hamburger stand to buy dinner for all of them, but she hadn't done that lately.

Toby came into the kitchen and stretched. Then he checked his food bowl, which was empty. "Morning, Tobe," Matt said casually. He was ninety-nine percent positive everything he thought had happened really had. But he didn't want to say anything about Toby's talking or about going to the Browns' until someone else did. Just in case it had all been a dream, he didn't want Kate laughing at him and telling their mother.

"Morning," Toby answered. Matt thought he saw a look of relief pass over Kate's face, too.

"Sorry, Toby," Matt said, opening the cabinet. "No more dog food. We're out. But I think there's some macaroni and cheese left from night before last. I could heat it up in the toaster oven."

Toby wagged his tail. "Sounds great, and don't bother heating it," he said cheerfully.

Matt scraped the macaroni into Toby's bowl and filled the empty pot with warm water. It bothered him that there wasn't a lot of food in the refrigerator. They were out of shampoo, too, and he had

28

had to use a bar of soap on his hair. Matt worried when they started running out of things around the house. He hated to ask his mother for money to buy things, because he was afraid she didn't have enough to spare.

When everyone had finished eating, Matt put Kate's bowl and the dirty glasses in the sink, and they all went outside. Matt locked the door carefully and put his key back around his neck. He knew their mother would be getting up soon to dress for work, but he didn't like to leave her sleeping with the door unlocked, even for a few minutes. "Okay," he called to Toby and Kate. "Let's go."

Mr. Brown had already left for work, but Mrs. Brown was sitting on the front steps of their house, reading the newspaper. When the children got close to the yard, Toby ran ahead, barking. He made a normal barking sound, but Matt and Kate thought that he was probably calling to Polly.

A moment later Polly pushed open the screen door and came out onto the porch. She growled softly and let the long fur on the back of her neck stand up. Then Toby barked again, and wagged his tail, and Polly relaxed and stopped growling.

29

"Hey, girl," Mrs. Brown said, standing up. "It's just the Baker kids here to say hello. Hey, kids."

"Hi, Mrs. Brown," Kate called. Matt unlocked the gate, and they all went into the yard. Polly ran to Toby and nosed around him in a friendly way, her tail wagging. She was much smaller than he, with short legs and thick, silky black-and-white fur. She looked like a very small, blunt-nosed collie.

Matt glanced around the yard, trying to seem casual. "We came to see the puppies, Mrs. Brown," he explained. Kate looked at him in surprise. She would sometimes tell a fib or even an outright story, but Matt hardly ever did.

When Matt said "puppies," Polly looked up at him sharply and whined. Then she rubbed against his legs and licked the palm of his hand.

Mrs. Brown smiled and shrugged. "Polly's not usually so friendly," she commented. "She must like you, Matt. Anyhow, children, I'm sorry, but the pups are gone. We gave them all away not a week ago."

"Yeah?" Kate said. "Who took them?"

Mrs. Brown looked at her, puzzled.

"Kate means," Matt broke in, "did one person adopt all the dogs, or did they go to different places?"

"Oh," Mrs. Brown said. "Why, they all went to the same place, to a lovely farm up north of here. They are going to be working dogs, except the littlest pup, the one we call Ranger. The woman who took the puppies liked him so much, she decided to keep him as her own house dog." Mrs. Brown smiled triumphantly. "Lucy," she said. "That was her name."

When Mrs. Brown said "Ranger," Polly barked twice and jumped off the porch. She looked around the yard and sniffed the sidewalk. Mrs. Brown called to her, but Polly ignored her and lay down on the walk. She put her nose on top of her folded paws and sighed.

"Well," Matt asked, "who was she? Whose farm was it? And how did she know you had puppies to give away in the first place?"

Kate had crouched down beside Polly and buried her hands in the dog's soft fur. She was speaking softly to Polly when Mrs. Brown's sharp tone startled her and made her look up.

"Well, I suppose she read our ad in the *Gazette*," Mrs. Brown said. "What's all this about, Matthew?"

"I was just wondering," Matt answered hastily. "I mean, I wanted to know who took them because . . . I . . . uh—"

"*Toby* wanted to know," Kate broke in. "Because they're *his* puppies. His and Polly's."

Matt put his hands over his eyes and groaned. Then he realized Mrs. Brown was laughing.

"Kate," she said, "what a perfectly delightful idea! Whatever makes you think so?"

One thing Matt knew about Kate was that she didn't like it when adults got all sweet-voiced and said she was "delightful."

"I think so because it *is* so," Kate replied stubbornly. "Toby and Polly are married. And those are his puppies, and we . . . we wanted one of them."

"Kate!" Matt said.

"Kate!" Mrs. Brown said.

Toby yelped, and his tail wagged furiously.

Mrs. Brown looked at the two dogs, who stood side by side. An odd look crossed her face. "Well," she said slowly, "I believe those pups did resemble your Toby. Some of them are a pretty tan color that they surely didn't get from Polly. And your mother does let Toby run wild, doesn't she? But," she went on, "you kids should have spoken up sooner. We'd have been glad to give you one of the pups, or all of them, for that matter. We haven't room for a pack of dogs here, and we never intended for Polly to be a mother.

"Mrs. Brown," Matt began, "I wonder if that lady would let us have one of the pups, if we called and asked her. I mean, does a farm need four dogs? She'd probably be happy to spare one."

"Three," Mrs. Brown corrected. "She kept Ranger for the house, remember? So that left three for the farm. But I don't believe I'd want to ask her for one back, not after we gave them to her. A gift is a gift. You kids know that."

"They weren't yours to give," Kate said angrily.

"Kate." Matt's voice was gentle. "They were so. We didn't even know they were Toby's until . . ."

Mrs. Brown smiled at Matt. "Until what, Matt?"

"Never mind," he mumbled.

Mrs. Brown bent down and picked up her paper. "I've got to get on in the house, children," she said. "I don't mean to shoo you away, but right now I've got to get back inside and finish my paper."

Matt knew that was Mrs. Brown's way of asking them to go home.

"Please, Mrs. Brown," he said. "If our mother said we could have one of the puppies, couldn't you call the lady—Lucy—for us? Please?"

Kate got up and stood next to Matthew. She folded her hands in front of her the way her

33

teacher said little girls ought to, and she gave Mrs. Brown a sweet, shy smile. "Yes, ma'am," she said in a baby voice. "Would you, please?"

Matt could hardly keep from laughing. He could never understand how Kate's goody-goody act could fool grown-ups. It didn't fool him at all. Sometimes she would do it just to make him laugh.

"Oh, honey," Mrs. Brown said. Her eyes got soft and tender-looking, and she smiled at Kate. "Tell you what. If your mommy says it's okay, I'll try to get hold of that woman and see if she could spare one dog. But I'm not promising anything, okay?"

"Okay, Mrs. Brown," Matt said. "Thanks." He tugged on Toby's collar. "Come on, Toby. Let's go home."

"Thank you, ma'am," Kate said sweetly. She giggled for absolutely no reason.

When the children were halfway home, Matt looked at Kate and gave her a sickly smile. "Oh, thank you, ma'am," he said, making his voice high-pitched.

Kate jumped up and down and held her arms over her stomach. She giggled the same silly way she had in Mrs. Brown's yard, and then she burst into loud, unladylike laughter and stuck her thumbs in her ears. "Oh, thank you," she said, wiggling her fingers around near her head.

Matthew and Kate laughed all the way home. After a while, even though he didn't know what was so funny, Toby began to laugh with them, barking and running in circles around the children as they walked down the hot sidewalk toward home.

Mrs. Brown thought about Matthew and Kate the whole time she was washing the dishes and sweeping the kitchen floor. She kept picturing the four puppies, and then Polly and Toby, and seeing how the kids might think the pups were his. When she finished sweeping, Mrs. Brown went into the bathroom and sprinkled cleanser all around the tub. Then she wiped down the sink with a sponge and picked up the wet towels off the floor.

There was something nagging at her, something in the back of her mind that she couldn't quite put her finger on. It had to do with the woman who had taken the puppies. She had said her name was Lucy, but she hadn't given her last name. And Mrs. Brown didn't think Lucy had left a phone number, either. Lucy had called Saturday morning and talked to Mr. Brown, then had come right to the house and taken the puppies away. She hadn't needed time to think about it at all.

Mrs. Brown sprayed glass cleaner on the medicine cabinet mirror and wiped it down. Then she put the top back on the toothpaste tube and turned off the bathroom light.

That was unusual, for someone to take four puppies and not even need to think it over first. There was something else about Lucy that was bothering Mrs. Brown. Lucy had been very nicely dressed. Mrs. Brown remembered that clearly because she herself had still been in her bathrobe, and she'd felt a little embarrassed. Lucy had nice long, pink fingernails, and she wore lots of gold rings. The rings called attention to her soft, pretty hands.

Soft, pretty hands. Surely Lucy wouldn't have such soft, pretty hands if she lived on a farm. Farmers had to work all the time, didn't they? Even if Lucy had a husband who did all the heavy work, wouldn't she still have to keep a garden and gather eggs and . . . and . . .

Mrs. Brown was pretty sure a farmer wouldn't have ten perfect long, pink fingernails.

But that didn't prove anything. Lucy could have wanted the dogs for a friend's farm. That was probably it. It seemed odd, though, that she wouldn't have said so. And if the dogs were for a friend, well, Mrs. Brown thought, someone might surprise a friend with one puppy—but with three? That didn't seem very likely.

Mrs. Brown went in the bedroom and picked the heavy spread up off the floor. She threw it over the bed and tucked it up under the pillows. While she was working, Polly came into the room and jumped up on the bed, which was forbidden. Mrs. Brown didn't have the heart to scold her, though. She picked Polly up in her arms and kissed her fur. Instead of licking Mrs. Brown's face or struggling to get away, Polly just whined softly and snuggled close.

"Maybe we should have kept one of those puppies," Mrs. Brown whispered into Polly's coat. "Wanda, maybe, to keep you company when Mr. Brown and I are away."

Polly gave Mrs. Brown's chin a swipe with her pink tongue. It was the only way she knew to show that she agreed with all her heart.

Chapter Four

Mrs. Baker was waiting when the children got home. She had finished her coffee and spread out some papers on the kitchen table. When she heard the kids at the back door, she stood up and swept the papers into her briefcase.

"My goodness, you guys are up early," she said, pulling Kate close for a kiss. "Hi, honey," she told Matt, ruffling his hair. "Feel better today?"

Matt nodded. "I gave Toby the last of the macaroni and cheese," he said. "Aren't you late for work?"

Mrs. Baker nodded. "I just wanted to kiss you

guys before I leave," she said. "I'll probably be late tonight. I've got the dentist at three, and then I've got to be back at the office for a four-thirty meeting. Are you sure you feel well enough to have Rusty over tonight?"

"Rusty!" Matthew exclaimed. "I forgot about him." Matt's cousin Rusty was coming over to have dinner and then spend the night.

"I hope you still want to," Mrs. Baker said, feeling around in the side pocket of her briefcase for her wallet. "Uncle Jim said he could drop Rusty here at four-thirty on his way downtown."

Jim Eddinger was a reporter for the *Los Angeles Gazette*. Sometimes he worked days, and sometimes nights. His son, Rusty, spent a lot of time at the Bakers' when Uncle Jim was on a story.

"Maybe it's not such a good night, after all," Mrs. Baker said doubtfully. "I'll be late, and there's nothing in the house for dinner. We could rearrange it for the weekend, couldn't we?"

"Mom," Matt protested. "You *promised*. Kate and I can go to the store and get everything we need. Just tell us what to get, okay?"

Mrs. Baker fished twenty dollars out of her wallet. "Okay," she agreed. "Go to the store. Just get milk, cereal, bananas, and, uh—"

"Bread," Kate broke in. "Cookies, butter, and dog food."

"Okay," Mrs. Baker replied, taking another twenty from her wallet. Matt was relieved to see that there was plenty of money in her purse. "And then use this to go to the hamburger stand and get dinner. A plain cheeseburger for me, large fries, and no drink, okay? Get whatever you want for the three of you. Don't go until after five-thirty. And don't forget to feed Toby!"

Matthew loved to watch his mother get ready to run out the door. She was always late for work, every day—or at least she said she was. When she threw on her jacket or sweater and gathered up her briefcase, her purse, and her lunch, she reminded Matt of the picture of Mary Poppins from one of Kate's books. She would have two or three things under one arm, and her keys in her hand, and she'd be trying to see herself in the hall mirror, and feeling her pockets for bus change, and calling out instructions to Matthew and Kate, all at the same time. Sometimes she'd make it out the door and halfway down the block before she remembered something she had to have, a book or her watch or a hairbrush. Then she'd come flying back into the house, still tossing out instructions, and Matt and Kate would have to run to help her.

Now Kate looked at Matt happily. "Mmm, hamburgers," she said, rubbing her stomach.

Mrs. Baker kissed the children again and went out the door. Matt waited until she was out of sight. Then he whistled for Toby, who had gone into the kitchen to check his food dish again.

"Okay," Matt said. "We've got work to do. First off, we've got to figure out how to get Mrs. Brown to find that Lucy's name and phone number."

"But, Matt," Kate argued, "she said to have Mom call her, and you know Mom won't. She's told us ten times no more dogs."

Toby sniffed. "I'm sure if Gretchen knew that these are *my* puppies we're discussing, she'd be pleased to take one. At *least* one."

Matt looked at Kate and shook his head ever so slightly, warning her not to contradict Toby. The dog seemed to get his feelings hurt awfully easily.

"Listen," Kate said. "We'll call up Mrs. Brown, and I'll pretend to be Mom. I'll put a handkerchief over the receiver so she can't hear me too well, and I'll say I've got what Miss Tyler had last year, when she was sick."

"Rabies?" Toby asked fearfully.

Kate shook her head impatiently. "You know, where you have to whisper everything."

"Oh," Matt replied. "You mean *laryngitis*, Kate."

Toby nodded. "Like kennel cough."

"Anyway, Kate," Matt said, "I don't really think that would work. Mrs. Brown knows your voice. What if she gets suspicious and wants to come over and see Mom personally? You know what kind of trouble we'll be in if Mom catches us in a lie like that!"

Kate frowned. "I could say I'm Mom's secretary," she offered, but Matt shook his head.

"We've got to think up something better," he told her.

"Well," Toby suggested, "why don't we ask Sergeant to take you over to Lucy's apartment building? He could point her out to you, and then you could talk to her and see if she's got the puppies."

Matt threw his arms around Toby's neck and hugged him. "That's a terrific idea," he said. "How do we find him?"

Toby lifted his ears and thought for moment. "He's usually at the supermarket about one o'clock," he said, "looking through the trash bins. Then he heads over to Poinsettia Park to chase bicycles."

"Well," Matt said, "it's nine-thirty now. We'll

wait till twelve and then go to the store. We've got to get the groceries, anyway."

"Good," Kate said. "Then I won't miss *The Jetsons* at eleven."

Matt gave Kate the choice of going inside the store to buy the groceries or going with Toby to look for Sergeant.

Kate bit her lip. "If you buy the groceries, what kind of cookies are you going to get?"

"Come on, Kate, what difference does it make? I'll get whatever kind you want."

"Okay," Kate agreed, testing him. "Raisin bars." She knew raisin bars were the only cookies Matt didn't like.

"Anything but," Matt argued. "Chocolate-chip cookies, okay? Or chocolate-covered grahams."

Toby lifted his muzzle. "I think I smell Sarge now."

A baby sitting in a stroller in front of the supermarket doors looked up when Toby spoke, then burst into tears. "Don't cry, boo-boo," the child's mother said, picking him up. "Big doggie won't bite you. Bad boy! Bad boy!"

The woman shook her finger at Toby. Kate looked at Matt in disgust. "Oh, brother," she grumbled.

"Doggie talk," the baby said clearly.

"That's right," the mother agreed. "Doggie talking."

For a moment Matt was startled, but then the woman went on. "Barking is doggie's way to say hello!"

"Yeah," Kate muttered. "And biting is doggie's way to say good-bye."

The woman looked at Kate and frowned. "I beg your pardon," she said politely. "Did you speak to me, little girl?"

Matt grabbed Kate's arm and gave her a push toward the trash bins in back of the store. "Go with Toby," he told her. "And don't pet a strange dog, hear me? Even if Toby knows him. Just wait for me."

Toby looked at Matt and blinked as though his feelings were hurt. "I'd never let Kate do anything dangerous, Master," he said. "Matt, I mean."

The woman shook her finger again. "No wonder my child is frightened," she said angrily. "That horrible dog just barks his head off, doesn't he?"

Matt turned his back on Kate and Toby, hoping they'd have enough sense to go. He gave the lady his most apologetic smile and went into the store.

45

As the automatic door closed behind him, he heard the baby speak again.

"Doggie talk! Doggie talk!"

When Matt came out of the supermarket, he left the bag of groceries tucked away behind the ice machine and went around back. Toby had said Sergeant was a German shepherd, but somehow Matt hadn't expected him to be so big. He seemed as broad as a wolf at the shoulders, and he was lean, with a shaggy gray coat. It was a hot day, and Sergeant's mouth was half open in a fierce grin as he panted to cool off. His teeth were yellow and sharp. He must have discovered some treasures in the trash bin, because there were torn wrappers and a few half-eaten cupcakes on the concrete beneath his feet.

Toby and the big shepherd were deep in a growled conversation. "He says he'll be glad to take us," Toby reported, wagging his tail as Matt came closer.

"Kate," Matt called, "come over here right now."

Toby took Kate's hand gently in his mouth and tugged. Reluctantly she let go of Sergeant's coat and went to stand by Matthew.

Sergeant waved his bushy tail in a friendly way,

but Matt held tight to Kate's hand. "Hear him growl?" he asked her. "Never, never, pet a growling dog."

Sergeant looked up at Matt and grinned wolfishly. Without meaning to, Matt backed up a step, and Toby moved between him and the shepherd. Toby gave a sharp, angry yelp, and Sergeant put his tail between his legs and moved a step away.

"He doesn't mean any harm," Toby explained. "Sergeant is a young dog, and he likes to play. I'm afraid he doesn't get much chance to play doggish games where he lives. Not," he added hastily, glancing at Sergeant, "that his mistress isn't a fine lady. But she's, well, old. She doesn't enjoy play fights, or even fetch-the-ball."

Matt whistled softly and patted his thigh. "Sorry, Sarge," he said softly. "Good dog."

The shepherd put his tail up, and his brown eyes seemed friendly and understanding. As he trotted away, he looked back over his shoulder questioningly.

"He's ready when we are," Toby said. "Let's go!"

Toby was right. Wilshire Boulevard was busy and loud and not at all pleasant. Kate wasn't scared, but she could see how a dog might be. The cars rushed by so fast, it could be awfully confusing.

Kate was hot and thirsty, and her sneaker had worn a blister on her left heel. It had been a long, hot walk from the store. Sergeant had shown them where the building was, but he didn't have any idea, Toby said, when Lucy would be coming out, or going in if she was already out.

The building was red brick with shiny brass fixtures on the doors and windows. There was a green cloth awning hung along the front walk, and a bright brass sign on the door that read: No Dogs. No Peddlers.

"It's so hot," Kate complained, plopping down on the front steps in the shade of the awning. "And there's someone in there staring at us."

Matt glanced through the thick glass doors and saw a man in a brown uniform. "Looks like the doorman, Kate," he said. "Come on, let's sit somewhere else."

Kate got up with a sigh. She and Toby followed Matt a few doors down to a stoop that didn't look quite so fancy. Sergeant had disappeared around the back of the building. He said he was going to check the back door, but Toby thought he was probably investigating the garbage cans. The trouble was, people kept coming in and out of the building, and everyone stopped and looked at them.

So they wouldn't attract so much attention, the children and Toby moved down the block to the bench by the bus stop.

"I don't know how we're supposed to recognize Lucy if she does come out," Kate said. "Where's Sergeant?"

Matt shrugged. "So far nobody's come in or out of Lucy's building," he replied. "So it doesn't matter." Just then he felt something wet nudge the inside of his hand. Sergeant licked Matt's palm and whined. Then he looked toward the building and woofed softly.

"Her car's not in the garage," Toby translated. He had been lying in the shade under the bench, but now he came out and danced around in a little circle, excited. "So she might come driving up anytime!"

Matt wiped the back of his hand over his forehead. His shirt was sticking to his chest, and he thought he'd do anything for a cold milk shake. "Anytime," he said wearily. "That could be hours from now."

Kate looked up. The sun was an orange ball low in the sky. "Well," she commented, "if Lucy

49

works in an office, she probably comes home same time as Mom. Five-thirty or six, right?''

Matt ignored her, daydreaming about that tall, cold shake. Only Toby and Sergeant kept their eyes steadily on the apartment building.

''Except,'' Kate went on, ''Mom won't be home by six today. She has to go to a meeting, remember?'' Kate stopped suddenly and clapped her hand to her mouth. ''Oh, no,'' she breathed. ''We forgot about Rusty!''

Milk shakes, Matt thought dreamily. ''Milk!'' he shouted suddenly. ''Bread, butter, and dog food. Kate, we forgot the groceries! The bag's still behind the ice machine at the grocery store.''

''*You* forgot them, you mean,'' Kate said.

''Oh, brother,'' Matt groaned. ''I wonder what time it is. If it's after four, we're sunk. We'll never get home before Uncle Jim drops Rusty off. Mom'll kill us.''

''Oh, no,'' Toby broke in. ''She won't do *that*. The worst she might do is spank you with the newspaper and make you go outside.''

Toby was trying to be helpful, but when he saw the look on Matt's face, he trotted over to stand by Sergeant. Sometimes it was easier to get along with dogs than with humans.

A moment later Sergeant broke into furious

barking. Now that Matt knew him, he was only a little frightened. "It's her car," Toby translated. "Ruff, ruff, woof! Row! Row-ow-ow-ow-ow!"

"Toby," Matt said, "please speak English!"

Toby jumped up on the bench and shouted over Sergeant's barking. "He says it's her, all right. It's Lucy! And look, she's getting out of the car. He swears by Sirius it's the same lady. He can smell her from here."

"Sergeant!" Matt called sharply. "Quiet! We don't want to attract any attention."

Someone in the building behind the children threw open a window. "Shut those mutts up," he yelled. "I'll call the cops!"

Another window flew open. "It's a pack of wild dogs," a woman screamed. "They're attacking some children right outside. Someone call the pound!"

Matt whirled around, trying to call to the woman to let her know they were all right. But his voice couldn't be heard over the barking and shouting.

Toby jumped off the bench, threw his front paws against Matt's chest, and gave his face a big, wet lick, trying to show the woman he was friendly.

"They're attacking," the woman screeched. "A pack of vicious pit bulls!"

By now people up and down the block were put-

51

ting their heads out of windows and yelling to one another. Sergeant was nearly hysterical with excitement. "Rowr! Rowr! Rowr!" he barked, as Toby translated.

"Lucy's leaving her car," Toby shouted, "and Sergeant says the smell of dog is all *over* that car. Sarge smells a hundred dogs, a *thousand*. He smells Ranger, and Wanda, and he thinks he can pick up Preston's scent, and Hal's, too!"

Of course, to the people coming out of the buildings Toby's barking sounded just like Sergeant's. "What's going on out there?" someone called, and across the street someone else answered.

"It's a pack of starved coyotes come out from the canyons. They're attacking children!"

"They've already gotten one child," a woman screamed. "A darling little girl. She was here just a moment ago, and now she's gone. I believe they've eaten her alive."

Matt's stomach made a funny flip-flop. He'd had that feeling before, and it nearly always concerned homework, tests, or Kate. He glanced around him wildly, but the woman was right. Kate was nowhere to be seen.

"Toby," Matt shouted. "Where's Kate?"

Toby whirled around, sniffed, and barked right in Sergeant's ear. Matt didn't know it, but Toby had almost exactly the same unpleasant sensation in his own stomach, only Toby thought of it as the "bad dog" feeling.

Sergeant heard the sirens first, and he yelped a warning to Toby. Then he took off like a streak of gray lightning across the manicured lawn, around a corner, and out of sight. "Trouble," Toby panted miserably, and then Matt heard the sirens, too.

"Run!" Matt shouted. "Toby, run! Go home, go anywhere!"

"But what about Kate?" Toby protested. People were still shouting from the apartments above them. Toby looked up at the sea of angry human faces, and then he looked down Wilshire Boulevard. A police car was speeding down the hill with its siren on and lights flashing.

"Run!" Matt shouted again. "Toby, *go home*."

And then, before Matt knew exactly what had happened, Toby was gone, and a tall, kind-looking policeman was leaning over him.

Oh, no, Matt thought.

"She was a *darling* little girl," a woman was saying. "I'm sure they ate her. The most *darling* little thing."

"Son," the police officer said, laying his big hand on Matt's shoulder. "What seems to be the trouble?"

Chapter Five

Kate hadn't had time to think about what she was going to do. When Lucy had gotten out of her car, leaving the door open, everyone, including the doorman and Lucy herself, had been watching Matt try to calm the hysterical dogs. No one had seen Kate back away and walk to Lucy's car. She had slipped into the backseat through the open door.

At first it had been a little scary, curled up on the floor behind the front seat. It seemed to take a long time before someone came and got into the car. Kate didn't realize why Lucy had left her car door open and the motor running. She had expected Lucy herself to come back and hop in the car, and when she opened her eyes and peeked under the front seat, she was surprised to see a large brown shoe, a man's shoe, resting on the brake pedal.

For a moment Kate thought about jumping up and yelling as loud as she could. Maybe this man had seen her sneak into the car and was kidnaping her, or taking her to the police station. But before she could decide what to do, the big brown shoe slid over to the gas pedal, the radio blasted to life, and the car took off.

Kate crossed her fingers on both hands. She uncurled her body as slowly as she could and edged onto the space of floor directly behind the two front seats. She could see the man's legs through the split between the seats. It looked as though he was wearing a uniform. Police, she thought. I'm in trouble, now. But why would a policeman drive Lucy's car away, and if he knew Kate was hiding in the back, why hadn't he said anything? Besides, Kate didn't think a policeman would like rock music, either. At least, not as loudly as it was blaring.

Kate pressed her face into the space between the two seats. She could just see the edge of the man's profile and the crisp brim of his brown hat. It didn't look like a policeman's hat, and his uniform didn't look like a policeman's uniform, either. Kate bit her lip hard, thinking. The doorman! This man's uniform was exactly like the doorman's uniform at Lucy's building.

Kate thought they must have driven five or six blocks already. They had certainly turned a lot of corners. She turned her head slightly and peeked out the window and was surprised to see they were passing Lucy's building. Before Kate could think what the driver was doing, he guided the car around another corner and pulled up in front of a steep driveway. At the base of the drive were two heavy metal doors.

Suddenly the man turned around, reaching his arm over the back of the seat, and Kate threw herself back down against the floor.

"Now where are you?" the man said, patting the backseat above Kate. His sleeve brushed the top of her head. She was about to swallow her fear and sit up when he suddenly took his arm away. "*There* you are," he said happily. A moment later Kate heard the heavy door below them roll open. The car eased down the drive. The man must have been looking for the automatic door opener, she thought with relief. He hadn't seen her at all.

The car rolled to a stop, and the man sighed happily. "Oh, you're some car," he said, patting the dashboard. "You're some baby. I'm gonna have me one like you someday, you doll."

Kate tried not to laugh. The man had been driving around and around the block, pretending the car was his own. It must be his job to park the cars for all the rich people in the building. Finally he turned off the ignition and opened the door. Kate held her breath as his heavy weight left the car and the door slammed shut. She counted—one hippopotamus, two hippopotamus—all the way to fifty, without cheating, to give him time to walk away. Then she sat up and peeked out the window. She was alone in a dim corner of a deserted underground parking garage.

The tall police officer had a patient face, but Matt thought that even this man might lose his patience if he didn't answer soon. "I asked you, son," the officer said again, "what seems to be the trouble here?"

Matt looked at his shoes and then all around him, at the tall buildings and the traffic rushing down Wilshire Boulevard. He couldn't find an answer anywhere. It would probably be best, he decided, to trust this kind-faced man and tell him the truth. At least, that way he'd get some help in finding Kate. Of course, their mother would have to be called, and Matt would have some serious explaining to do. Mom would probably send Kate off to day camp and make Matt go, too. Unless, of course, she decided to send them both off to the looney bin. Nobody was going to believe them about the dog's talking, that was for sure. So far Matt hadn't come across anybody but Kate and the little baby at the supermarket who could understand Toby. At best he'd probably be grounded for the rest of the summer, and they'd never find out what had happened to Toby's puppies.

Matt squared his shoulders and cleared his throat. "Um, you probably won't believe this, but here goes. See, I came down here with my dog and my—"

"Matt," Toby barked. "Here I am, here I am!"

The policeman whirled around, but relaxed when he saw Toby's friendly grin and wagging tail.

"Here, boy," Matt said, relieved.

"Control that dog, son." The policeman spoke sternly. "Have you got a leash for him, and a license?"

Matt turned pale. "Yes, sir," he said hastily. "I sure do, only they're at home. See, I opened the front door of my house to . . . to get the mail for my mother, and Toby saw a cat and ran out, and

I ran out after him, and he took off so fast, it was all I could do to just keep up with him. I chased him all the way down here, and I just now caught him!''

Toby barked agreeably and wagged his tail.

''So you live around here, son?'' the officer asked. ''Where, exactly?''

''Well,'' Matt answered slowly, ''right up at Santa Monica and Laurel.''

''Santa Monica and Laurel!'' The policeman threw back his head and laughed. ''You chased that dog all the way down here? That's nearly two miles away.''

''Yes, sir,'' Matt agreed. ''And now I caught him, and I've got to get him home before my mom starts to get worried.''

''Don't worry about that, son,'' the policeman said. ''I'm going to call your mother and let her know you're just fine. And then we'll check that license you've got at home, too, and make sure that's in order.''

Matt turned even paler. ''My mother? But I— I—'' he stuttered.

''Now,'' the officer went on. ''What's all this about a little girl being eaten by dogs? This old fellow doesn't look like he'd hurt anybody,'' he said, bending over to scratch behind Toby's ears. "Easy now, boy."

"I don't know anything about any little girl," Matt replied weakly. "I mean, I saw one, but I don't think she got *eaten*. I mean, I *know* she didn't. She . . . she went into that building over there." Matt pointed, and the police officer looked up with interest. "With her mother and father, I think. But I don't know, exactly, because I don't know her. The little girl, I mean. I just happened to notice her while I was chasing my dog."

The policeman nodded in an encouraging way. He had arrested a lot of criminals in his time, and he knew when a suspect was acting guilty. This kid certainly was.

"Please," Matt blurted out. "Don't call my mother! She's not home. I lied about that. I'm supposed to be home, watching my—"

Toby barked a warning, and Matt bit his tongue.

"My *dog*," he finished awkwardly. "I'm supposed to be watching my dog, and my mom said if he runs out the door one more time, she'll send him to the pound." Matt swallowed hard. "*Please*," he said again.

The police officer scratched his head and frowned. No wonder the poor kid was so frightened. His mother had threatened to have his dog put away. Some people!

"Okay, son. Let's stay calm, now. Nobody's going to take your dog away."

Matt sniffed and wiped at his eyes with the back of his hand, trying to make it look as if he were just scratching. Toby wagged his tail and whined softly. He didn't understand everything the policeman was saying, but he got the gist of it. He tried his best to look like a *good dog*.

"I don't see any reason why we have to call your mother," the officer continued, "if you'll slip your belt under this fellow's collar to make a leash and walk him straight home." Matt grinned happily, and the policeman signaled his partner over the top of Matt's head.

"And don't let him run loose," he went on. "It's not safe, you know, and there's a law against it, too."

"Yes, sir," Matt said respectfully, slipping his belt under Toby's collar. "Come on, Tobe." Matt pulled on the leash. He wanted to get away before the policeman changed his mind.

"Matt," Toby protested, "what about Kate? We can't leave without her!"

Matt gave the leash another tug, and Toby followed reluctantly.

"And, son, keep that animal quiet, would you please?"

It was Matt's plan to keep walking until he was sure the police car had driven away. Then, he figured, he would turn around and go back to look for Kate. The first thing he had to do, though, was to get away from the nosy policeman and his questions. He headed toward the bus stop where he and Kate had waited earlier. A city bus sat waiting with its engine running and its front door open.

The policeman watched the boy and the dog until they'd reached the corner. Then he got into his car, and his partner took off, sliding the car into the busy traffic. If he had turned away a moment sooner, he wouldn't have noticed the dark-haired girl running out of the apartment building, and the doorman staring after her, bewildered.

"Matt!" Kate shouted. "Wait for me!"

"Master!" Toby yelped. "It's Kate! We've found her!"

Matt turned around, frantically whispering to Toby to be quiet and act as though he didn't recognize Kate. If the policeman were watching, he would know Matt had lied and he'd surely want to ask the kids some more questions.

For a moment Matt thought they were safe. Then

he saw the black-and-white car cut across three lanes of traffic toward the curb where he and Toby stood.

"Matt!" Kate was approaching Matt at an alarming rate. She had some papers in one hand. "Wait up! Wait up!"

Matt had to act fast. The patrol car had pulled up at the curb twenty feet away, and the passenger door was swinging open. "Come on, Toby," Matt shouted. He grabbed Kate's wrist and swung her around so that they were all running in the direction she had just come from.

"Matthew," Kate protested, panting hard. Her hair was drenched in sweat, and she wanted to stop and take a few deep breaths. Matt was making her run too fast; he always did that.

"Kate, come on!" Matt pushed Kate in front of him into the waiting bus. Then he yanked on Toby's leash and pulled him on board, too. A moment later the doors heaved shut and the bus pulled away from the curb. Matt watched the confused policeman put one hand on his forehead to shield his eyes from the sun. The policeman turned in a slow circle and looked all around. His eyes barely brushed the bus as it lumbered out onto Wilshire Boulevard.

"Ouch!" Kate said grouchily. "You don't have

to *push*. Don't you even want to know where I was all that time? I hid out in Lucy's car, Matt. And I—"

"Kate, be quiet," Matt said impatiently. "Do you have any change? I have a dollar bill, but we need another ten cents."

"No," the bus driver corrected, "you don't. You don't need to pay me at all."

"Wow," Matt said gratefully. *"Thanks."*

"You don't need to pay me," the bus driver said firmly, "because you're getting off the bus." He had a round, brown face that looked friendly, but his words didn't sound friendly at all. "No dogs allowed on this bus."

But the bus was still lumbering down the street. Matt hoped they could ride another block before the driver made them get off.

Kate got up and took the leash from Matt's hand. "This is my guide dog," she said with dignity. "I am blind."

Matt covered his face with his hands. Now he couldn't wait to get off the bus.

The bus driver glanced away from traffic for just a moment and looked at Kate. Then he smiled and shook his head. "That's fine," he said agreeably, turning back to the windshield. "As long as you're not *deaf*, so you can hear me tell you that you've got to get *off* this bus.''

''This is my guide dog,'' Kate said again. ''Matthew, please pay the driver. It's hot outside, and I will not walk another *step* in this terrible heat.''

Pulling Toby along behind her, Kate made her way to the seat behind the driver. Luckily, the bus was nearly empty, because Toby didn't have any idea how a guide dog should act. He sprawled out in the middle of the aisle and sighed contentedly. It felt good to get his paw pads off the hot cement.

''We'll get off,'' Matt said dejectedly. ''Sorry.''

The bus driver turned and gave Matt a knowing look. ''That's your sister, huh? Gotta look out for her?''

Matt nodded.

''Tell you what,'' the driver said softly. ''How far you going?''

''Up Fairfax,'' Matt answered. ''To Santa Monica Boulevard.''

''Well,'' the driver said, ''that child's no more blind than I am. And *I'm* driving the bus. But I can see she's hot and tired, and that mutt looks about beat.''

Matt wiped his forehead on his sleeve. He was hot and tired, too.

''Now, it's against the rules,'' the driver went

on, "for that dog to ride. No two ways about it. But I suppose if you want to stand here and argue with me about it till we get up to Santa Monica Boulevard, then what am I gonna do? I can't *put* you off the bus. Anybody complains, well, I have to tell 'em I told you take the dog off, and you just wouldn't do it."

Matt grinned. "Thanks," he said, digging into his pocket for the fare.

"Forget that, kid," the driver said. "I ain't lettin' you ride, remember? So why should you have to pay?" And then he called out, in a louder voice, "Next stop, Beverly!"

When they got off the bus, Matt gave the driver a friendly smile. Toby wagged his tail gratefully. And Kate lifted her hand delicately and waved in the wrong direction, as if she couldn't see him.

"Kate," Matt said. He sounded disgusted. "Will you come on, and stop being such a *baby*?" He didn't notice Kate's hurt expression. "I wish I knew what happened to Sarge," he added, sounding worried. "I hope he makes it home okay."

Toby made a funny sound deep in his throat. "Matt, Sergeant knows his way around the city as if it were the puppy farm he grew up on. You don't have to worry about him."

"I guess," Matt replied. "Come on, you guys. Let's see if the groceries are still there. We'll have to rush home and try to get there before Rusty and Uncle Jim. Too bad," he went on, "we didn't have time to snoop around a little more. I mean, yeah, we found out from Sarge that Lucy's definitely the same one who took the puppies, and that she lives in a no-dog building, not on a farm. But now what?"

"I know you'll find my pups, Matt," Toby said loyally.

"Thanks, Toby," Matt answered. "But I guess it was a big waste of time going down there. All we did was start a bunch of trouble."

"Well," Kate offered, "we found out Lucy's last name. And we found out where she works, too. At least," she added, "*I* did. But I guess I won't bother telling you, since I'm such a little *baby*."

They were at the entrance to the grocery store parking lot. Matt turned around and stared at Kate. "What?" he exclaimed.

Kate waved her pieces of paper in his face. "An envelope addressed to Lucy," she announced smugly. "And one of those little cards with her name and address on it. I took them out of her car. Her last name is S-I-M-O-N-S," she read.

"Simons," Matt said.

"That's what I *said*. And she works at the "Brem, Breem, B-R-E-M-E-R uh, lavatory."

"Laboratory," Matt corrected, "Bremer Laboratories. Kate, let me see those." He tried to snatch the paper out of her hand, but Kate danced away. "Nah, nah, nah, nah, nah," she taunted Matt, waving the papers at him, just out of reach.

Toby spoke up. "Please, Kate," he said gravely, and she was suddenly ashamed.

"I'm sorry," she told the dog, handing the business card to Matt. She stuffed the crumpled envelope into her pocket. Then she put her arms around Toby's neck and hugged him. "Come on, Matt," Kate said cheerfully. "Let's get the groceries. I'm starving!"

Matt examined the little white card Kate had taken from Lucy's car. Lucy Simons, it read. *Subject Procurement*.

Matt didn't know exactly what those words meant, but they gave him a funny, unpleasant feeling in the pit of his stomach. He shivered and followed Kate across the sparkling asphalt.

Chapter Six

❖

The milk was warm, but at least the bag of groceries was still where Matt had stashed it behind the ice machine at the supermarket. He handed Kate the chocolate-covered graham crackers, and she ripped the package open and handed cookies all around. The chocolate coating was melted, but no one minded. As thirsty as they were, they were hungry, too, and the cookies were sweet and delicious.

"Come on, we've got to hurry," Matt urged, and the others fell into step beside him.

"I say we get Mom to go over to Lucy's apartment with us and we just *demand* to know what she did with those dogs," Kate said, licking chocolate off her fingers.

"Oh, sure," Matt said. "Kate, look. We can't explain to anybody about Toby's talking, and being worried about the puppies, and all. You know that. We've got to figure out what to do ourselves."

"Well," Toby broke in, "I don't see why you didn't run up to her apartment as long as you were there, Kate, and sniff around a little. Maybe you would have picked up Ranger's scent, or Wanda's. Or Preston's, or maybe Hal's." Toby whined softly and tucked his tail between his legs.

Matt shifted the bag of groceries to his other arm and exchanged looks with Kate.

"I'm sorry, Tobe," Kate replied tactfully. "That would have been a good idea. But I don't know if I could have . . . um . . . picked up the scent. And besides, I was afraid you were worried about me."

Kate would have said more, but as they rounded the corner onto Laurel, they saw Uncle Jim's car parked in the driveway. He and Rusty had the motor running and the windows rolled up tight against the August heat.

"Where've you kids been?" Uncle Jim called, rolling down the window. "We've been waiting ten minutes. Where's your mother?"

"Sorry, Uncle Jim," Matt said. "Hi, Rusty. She's not coming home until late, maybe seven-thirty. She gave me money to take Rusty and Kate out for hamburgers."

"All *right*!" Rusty exclaimed. He was trying to ignore Kate, who was staring at him hatefully.

"Okay," Uncle Jim said. "Hop out, son. Take your knapsack." He patted his jacket pockets and finally found his wallet. "Here," he said, giving Matt another five. "Add this to what you have. You and Rusty treat Kate to a comic book or something. Got your house key?"

Matt stuck the money in his back pocket and grinned. "Yes, sir," he answered. "Thanks, Unc." The three children stood and watched until Rusty's father had driven away. Then they turned and went inside to put away the groceries.

"Come on, Matt," Rusty said as soon as they'd finished the bag of cookies. There was nothing good on television. "Let the kid stay here and baby-sit Toby, and we'll go down and get the hamburgers."

"No way!" Kate yelled. "I'm not a kid, and Toby doesn't need baby-sitting. He's a *dog*. That's just a phony excuse you made up 'cause you don't want me to go with you, but forget it, 'cause I'm

73

going." Her eyes were narrowed in anger. Kate *loathed* Rusty Eddinger. She didn't understand how someone as nice as Uncle Jim could have him for a son. "Besides," she said, "you're trying to get some of the five dollars, but Uncle Jim said it was mainly for me. I *heard* him. Right, Matt?"

"Sure, Kate," Matt agreed. "Don't worry, we'll get *two* comics for you, and whatever you want to eat. Double french fries, if you want, okay?"

"Matt!" Kate couldn't believe it. Matt always acted like that when Rusty was around, but it surprised her every time. She and Matt would be best friends all day, and then with Rusty there, he'd act as if she were just a little brat or something.

"Come on, Kate," Matt coaxed. He felt a tiny bit ashamed of himself. "You know you always end up crying if we take you anyplace. Every single time. Stay here, and you can watch any show you want. You'll have the place all to yourself, and we'll only be gone an hour, okay?"

"An *hour*," Kate wailed. "That means you're gonna eat there. It's not fair. You're not supposed to leave me alone—Mom said!"

"Awww," Rusty said, making an ugly face at Kate. "Poor little baby, afraid to stay alone. Goochie goochie goo, little baby. Goochie goochie goo."

Kate wanted to ignore Rusty, but she just couldn't. He was so mean and . . . and just *hateful*. "I'm not afraid," she yelled. "Shut up! Shut up!"

"Yeah, Rusty," Matt said. "Just shut up, okay? Kate, it's not even dark out. You're not scared to stay alone for a few minutes, are you?"

Kate felt her eyes get hot and fill with tears. She hated Rusty, and now she hated Matt, too. "I hate you," she yelled. "I hate hate, hate, hate YOU."

"Awww," Rusty said. "Goochie goochie goo!"

Kate jumped up and ran over to Rusty. She balled her hand up into a fist and smacked it into Rusty's stomach as hard as she could.

"OOOF!" Rusty yelled. "Hey, you little brat!" He took off after Kate, but she was too fast for him. She ran into the kitchen, letting the door slam behind her, and then she cut around through the dining room.

"Hey," Matt shouted. "Wait a minute. Rusty!"

Toby had had enough. He knew not to butt in when Kate and Matt had a fight. All they usually did was yell at each other. He didn't like it, but he'd just slink under the big cabinet in the living room and hide until it was over.

But this was different. Toby liked Rusty, although he tried to be standoffish for Kate's sake. But now Rusty was chasing Kate around the house, yelling at her. Toby couldn't understand every word, but he could catch enough. He barked twice and threw himself in front of the dining room door, blocking the boy's path.

"That's far enough." Toby showed Rusty his teeth.

"Hey," Rusty said, backing off. "Call off your mutt, Matt. What's the matter with him? He won't stop barking at me."

"I don't want to bite you," Toby told him, "but I will if I have to." He stood his ground, stiff-legged, with the yellow fur along his neck lifted into a sharp bristle.

"Come on, Matt," Rusty said. "Call him off, will you?" He put his hands palms up and shrugged. "Good boy," he said. "Good doggie. I wasn't going to hurt her."

Matt was staring at his cousin open-mouthed. "Rusty," he said at last. "Doesn't that even *surprise* you? That Toby's telling you to leave Kate alone?"

Rusty shrugged, still keeping an eye on the dog. "Why should it?" he asked. "Don't all dogs protect their owners?"

"But Rusty," Matt said. "That he's telling you, I mean. Talking to you like that. You act like it's something that happens every day—a dog says something, and you understand."

Kate had come around through the living room, and now she sat down next to Toby and put her arm around his neck. "Matt," she said. "He doesn't understand Toby."

"I understand him, all right," Rusty exclaimed. "He's about to take a chunk out of my leg!"

Matt looked at Toby in wonder. "But *Rusty's* not an adult. He's the same age as me—eleven."

Toby relaxed and sat down. He yawned and leaned against Kate. "I'm not surprised," he said disdainfully. "The same way that a few adults can understand us, there are always a few kids who can't. The old hounds say some kids are just born old."

"Tell your mutt to quit that yapping," Rusty said sullenly. "I'm not going to hurt your bratty little sister."

"Toby *talks*, Rusty," Kate said. "Whether you believe it or not. He talks in *words*. He's not *yapping*."

"Come on, Matt," Rusty groaned. "Do we have to sit around and play games with the little baby all night? Let's go get something to eat, okay?"

Matt shrugged, not looking at Kate and Toby.

"Okay," he agreed. "Um, what kind of milk shake do you want, Kate? Chocolate?"

Kate got up slowly and walked out of the kitchen. "Come on, Toby," she said coolly, ignoring the boys. Toby gave Matt a reproachful glance and followed her into the living room.

"A talking dog!" Rusty said as he and Matt went out the back door. "Give me a break!"

Then he said something else Kate couldn't quite catch, and both boys began to laugh. "Traitor," she said angrily. "You're nothing but a big, mean traitor."

It wasn't as much fun going to the hamburger stand with Rusty as Matt had thought it would be. He kept thinking about Kate, left home alone. The bag of burgers and fries he'd bought for his mother and Kate was stained with grease, and the food inside was cold. Besides that, Rusty kept reaching into the bag and stealing french fries. By the time they got to the store where Matt liked to buy his comic books, the fries were nearly gone.

"Come on, Rusty," Matt said impatiently. "Pick something out and let's go. We've got to get back before my mom gets home, or I'll really be in trouble."

"Okay, okay," Rusty answered, without closing

the comic he was flipping through. He liked to read one in the store before he paid for one. That way he got double his money's worth.

Matt had used Kate's share of Uncle Jim's five and most of his own to buy her a copy of *Elle*. It was her favorite, but their mother would never let her buy it, because she said it was too sophisticated for Kate to read. Kate liked to study the models' hair and makeup. But their mother said that was a waste of time *and* money. Matt gave Rusty his share of the five dollars, a dollar sixty-seven, and used the last of the change to buy three packs of Whoppers.

"Rusty," Matt said, grabbing the comic out of Rusty's hands, "come on! I've got to go right *now*."

"Oh, come on," Rusty replied. "Chill out, Matt."

"I'm quickly getting sick of you, Rusty," Matt said. He threw the half-read comic on the counter and snatched the money from Rusty's hands to pay for it.

"Hey, wait a minute," Rusty said, scooping his change off the counter. "I want to get some candy, Matt. Hang on!"

Matt ran out the swinging glass door, and a moment later Rusty followed. He muttered something under his breath, but Matt didn't hear him. They were mad at each other the whole way home, which was just as well, because running three blocks made them too out of breath to talk, anyway.

"Kate," Matt called, as he pushed the front door open. "Where are you? Come here, I've got a surprise for you!"

The house seemed ominously empty. Matt paused for a moment in the front hall, a little disturbed by the silence. Then he realized what was wrong—even if Kate was in her room sulking, Toby should have come running out to greet him.

"Toby?" Matt called. "Here, boy. Kate?"

Rusty took the greasy white bag from Matt's hands. "Good," he said. "A burglar probably broke in and got her. I might as well eat her burger."

"Put that down!" Matt yelled, grabbing the bag from Rusty. "Those hamburgers are for my mom and Kate, you jerk!"

"Relax, dude," Rusty said. "I wasn't gonna eat Aunt Gretchen's. Just the brat's."

"And she's not a brat," Matt replied angrily. Rusty followed him into the living room. "Kate?"

Kate wasn't in the dining room or the kitchen,

or in the bedroom she shared with their mother. Neither was Toby. Finally Matt checked his own room, and there, pinned to the unmade bed with a deck of cards, was a note from Kate.

Matt picked it up, his heart beating fast. Their mother would be home any minute. Matt knew he'd be in for it if she came home and Kate was gone.

> *Dear Matt*, (the note read)
> *the dear part is a joke, hah. hah. Me and Toby*
> *are finding the puppies. You'll be in worse*
> *trouble than me, Love, Kate.*

Matt groaned and stuck the note in his pocket.

"Come on, Rusty," he said, pulling a sweatshirt over his head.

It was a good thing they decided to go out the back door. Matt was just slipping out behind Rusty when he heard his mother's key in the front door. "Hello," she called. "Is anyone home? Kids?"

Matthew closed the door and locked it. Then he and Rusty sneaked around the side of the house, down the front steps, and out toward Fairfax Avenue.

Chapter Seven

✤

"My mother is going to kill me." Matt sounded hopeless. "My-mother-is-going-to-kill-me." No matter how he said it, it had the awful ring of truth.

"So," Rusty said, "find the kid. How far can she have gotten? Where could she be headed?"

Matt shook his head. "My mother will have the police out looking for us any minute," he replied. "She's probably already called your dad to make sure we're not there. She might check the hamburger place to be sure we're not hanging around, and then she'll panic and call the cops. I know my mom, believe me."

"So," Rusty said, "call her now, before she has a chance to panic. Tell her my dad took us all to a movie."

Matt stared at Rusty hopefully, but then his shoulders slumped. "Toby," he said. "What about Toby? We wouldn't have taken him to a movie, would we?"

Rusty thought for a minute, and then his face brightened. "A dog show," he offered. "Tell her my dad's covering a dog show for the paper, and he took us along. Toby, too."

"At night?" Matt asked doubtfully. But he couldn't think of anything better. He felt his pockets for change and took off running toward the telephone booth on the corner. A moment later he was talking to his mother, trying not to sound out of breath.

Rusty sauntered along the darkening street behind Matt, hoping this wouldn't somehow end up with his being in trouble, too. He'd probably get yelled at for teasing the kid. They'd blame it all on him and say he made her run away; Rusty just knew they would. He didn't mean any harm, anyway. He sort of liked her. It made him wish he had a sister to tease and play jokes on and stuff. It was fun.

"Yeah, Mom," Matt was saying nervously,

when Rusty reached the phone booth. "We're at Uncle Jim's. Sorry, I should have left you a note. Yeah, we took Toby, too. Uncle Jim said it was okay. Mmn-hmn. No—he . . . um . . . he went downstairs to . . . um . . . warm up the car. Kate? Yeah, she's okay. Yeah, I left your hamburger on the kitchen table." Matt wiped his forehead nervously and tried not to look at Rusty. He was afraid if he looked at Rusty, he'd laugh.

Finally Matt hung up. "Oh, boy," he said gloomily. "We're in for it now. My mother said to tell your dad to have us home by ten! If we don't find Kate and get home by then, we're sunk. Hey," he exclaimed. "Your dad isn't going to call my house, is he?" Matt's stomach gave a nasty little jump.

Rusty shook his head. "No way," he said. "He's working late at the newspaper tonight; that's why he let me spend the night."

Matt was hunting through his pockets for the little card Kate had stolen from Lucy's car earlier that day. "Okay," he said grimly. He squinted and held the card close to his face. "I think I have a good idea where they might be headed. It's, uh, 1000 Randall Road in Santa Monica. So that should be about ten blocks from the beach, I guess—around . . . uh . . . Lincoln. Right?"

Rusty shrugged. "I guess," he agreed. "But who's at 1000 Randall Road, Matt? Whose address is that?"

"Not who, Rusty," Matt corrected. "*What*. 1000 Randall Road is the address of Bremer Laboratories, where Lucy works. Remember when Kate was trying to tell you about Toby and his missing puppies and all? Well, Lucy's the person who took them. I mean, she didn't steal them, they were given to her. But maybe she tricked the Browns into giving them to her."

"Matt," Rusty said slowly, as if he were talking to somebody crazy, "what are you talking about?"

"Oh, forget it," Matt said. "I'll explain it on the bus. We've got to walk up to Santa Monica Boulevard and catch the number two. It goes all the way to the beach."

The cab driver looked at the little girl in his rearview mirror. "Okay, kiddo," he said. "We're almost there. Your dad gonna meet you?"

Kate frowned and pretended she hadn't heard him.

"Okay," the cab driver said, pulling up to the curb in front of the building. "Hop out. This is it."

Kate looked up and saw floor after floor of

square windows, some dark, and some lit from within.

"This *is* the place, isn't it, kid?"

Kate looked at the driver's face for the first time. He had worried-looking eyes and long yellow hair that stuck out from beneath his blue cap. "Mike" was spelled out in red letters across the front of the cap. He looked like a nice man.

If Kate was scared or upset and somebody looked at her in a kind way like Mike was, it usually made her burst into tears. So she scowled and looked at the meter. Seven dollars and eighty-eight cents! She dug in her pocket. She was going to have to use up almost all of the eight dollars she'd saved from her allowance.

"Here," she said. Then she remembered what her mother always told cab drivers. "Keep the change."

Mike smiled gratefully. "Thanks, miss," he said, "but kids ride half price."

He handed Kate back four dollars, and she took them, secretly relieved.

"Okay," he said. "Now, you and Fido hurry up and get inside, will you?"

"Toby," Toby said quietly, hopping out of the cab. "Not Fido."

Mike gulped and looked back at Kate, who

shrugged. "Well," she told him, "it's true. His name's Toby, not Fido."

Kate petted Toby's soft ears and watched the yellow cab pull away from the curb and disappear into the dark night.

"May I help you?"

The soft voice startled Kate. She hadn't seen the uniformed woman behind the security desk.

"May I help you?" the woman repeated. "Sorry, no dogs allowed in the lobby. Are you looking for someone?"

Kate let her hand rest on Toby's collar. "I . . . uh . . . I wanted to use the bathroom, please," she said, smiling sweetly.

The woman shrugged. "I'm sorry," she said, shaking her head. "Tell your mommy and daddy to try the service station up on Montana." She hesitated for a moment and smiled. "Did your dog want to use the rest room, too?"

Kate looked at the security officer blankly.

"There *is* someone waiting outside for you, isn't there, little girl? What's your name?"

"Katherine Justine Baker," Kate answered truthfully.

"Oh, sure," the guard said, surprising Kate. "Baker! You should have said so. Henrietta Baker up in research must be your mother. Then Kate remembered that Baker is a common name. She stroked Toby's head and smiled.

"I'll phone up and ask her to come down for you."

Kate swallowed hard. "Um, never mind," she said nervously. "She'll get mad if you bother her."

The woman smiled sympathetically and shrugged. "Sorry," she said again. "If I can't call your mom, you can't go up. Security reasons. I'd take you if I could, but I can't leave my desk. Maybe you'd better run back out and ask your dad to take you over to the service station after all."

Kate bit her lip and frowned. "Okay," she said at last. "Thanks anyway."

"Besides," the guard added, giving Kate a little wave with her fingers, "this building is no place for a nice dog like yours."

Toby growled very, very softly, and Kate tightened her hand on his collar as they went outside. He was shaking all over, and Kate realized suddenly that he was afraid.

"There's a very bad smell in there," Toby remarked, when they were in the shadows of the front walk again. "A terrible smell of trouble, and fear, and . . . and . . . *pain*."

Kate's eyes widened, and Toby whined, sorry

he had frightened her. He wished they hadn't sneaked out without Matthew. As much as he wanted to be sure his puppies were safe, still, he thought longingly of how it would feel to be curled up on the living room rug with his chin resting on Gretchen's feet, and the children safe in their rooms, asleep.

"Did you pick up the scent of the pups, Toby?" Kate asked.

Toby crouched low to the ground and tucked his tail between his hind legs. "I smelled a *hundred* pups in there, Kate," he replied grimly, making his voice as quiet as he could. "A hundred, a thousand, or *more*. Puppies and dogs and cats and rabbits." He looked up and met Kate's eyes. "It's not a pet store, is it?" he asked hopefully, but Kate shook her head.

"Or a petting zoo, or an animal farm?"

Kate shook her head again. "I'm not sure exactly what this place is, Toby," she said carefully. "But I don't think it's a good place at all." Then she brightened and gave Toby a reassuring pat. "Don't worry, Tobe. If your puppies are in there, we'll find them. We just have to think of how to get inside."

* * *

Rush hour was long over by the time Matt and Rusty got on, so the bus made good time. Matt spent the whole ride trying to convince Rusty that he wasn't just making up a wild story about the search for the puppies. Rusty liked a good story, and he liked an adventure even more, so he half believed Matt and half pretended to believe, just for the sake of fun.

The boys got off at Second Street and had turned the corner onto Randall Road. They were almost in front of the Bremer Laboratories building when the sound of shattering glass cut through the peaceful night. A moment later a shrill alarm began to sound. Matt yelled, ''Oh, no, that's *Kate*. She must have broken a window, and it set off an alarm.''

Sure enough, as the boys watched, a small girl and a medium-size dog crept around the side of the building. Just then a uniformed security guard came out the swinging glass doors. Matt raced after Kate, slipping past the guard as her back was turned. But Rusty hesitated, thinking that this adventure wasn't turning out to be so much fun after all.

Rusty watched as Kate and Toby tore through the brightly lit lobby to the bank of elevators with Matt just behind them. There was an elevator waiting, and they slipped into it. The doors shut immediately, but Rusty didn't panic. He'd seen this kind of elevator before, so he knew he could watch the red arrow over the doors to see where the three got off.

He watched as the arrow slid to one, then two, then three. Three. Good. He'd slip into the lobby and up the stairs and join them.

Rusty pushed open the glass door and was just walking into the lobby when a small, strong hand closed around the back of his collar.

"Okay, son," the woman said. "Hold it right there."

Rusty turned around slowly as the woman pushed him into the building. She had a walkie-talkie in her hand and a frightening shiny leather holster on her hip. "Ten-oh-six, cancel code yellow," she said into the walkie-talkie. "I caught him. A young fellow, too. Ten-four. Just one kid. I can handle it if you'll ring maintenance and tell 'em to board up the window.

"And now, young man," she said, sliding the walkie-talkie back onto her waistband, "suppose you tell me just what possessed you to toss a rock through that window?"

Chapter Eight

✤

Matt checked Lucy Simons's business card again. Then he punched the button for the third floor. Kate was scared to death, which meant she was refusing to talk softly or to tiptoe or to do almost anything else Matt suggested. And Toby was no help at all. He was huddled in the far corner of the elevator, shivering and looking around him. His nose twitched and quivered. Matt knew that the dog had caught a scent that frightened him very much indeed.

When the doors opened onto the third floor, Matt was relieved to see that the hallway looked abandoned. A dim light spilled from glass panes set into some of the doors, but the hall was empty and quiet.

"Come on," Matt whispered, grabbing Kate's hand. She snatched it away but stayed close beside him, anyway. "Come on, Toby," Kate said softly. "Come on, boy. Don't be afraid."

Toby wagged his tail bravely and followed the children. They would need him, he knew, to find the puppies if they were somewhere behind one of these closed doors. As Matt and Kate crept down the hall, Toby stopped at the first door and inhaled deeply. The sharp odor of chemicals burned the tender inside of his nose, and he backed away hastily. "No puppies there," he growled softly. "No humans, either."

At the next door Toby stopped and sniffed again. "Chemicals," he woofed. "Smells like that stuff Mom pours on the kitchen floor."

"Shh," Matt warned.

"I don't think they're on this floor," Toby answered, as quietly as he could. "I just smell chemicals. It's not a very nice smell, either." He padded to the next door and thrust his muzzle against the doorjamb. Then he ran to the next door and did the same thing.

While Toby was picking up scents, Matt got on one knee and put the other one up to make a step

94

for Kate. She got up and looked through the glass into the dimly lit room.

"It's just an office," she said. "Desks and stuff, and some filing cabinets. This doesn't look like any lab I've ever seen. There's some pictures of girls on the walls, with a lot of makeup and stuff on, and a big picture of a man's hand holding a test tube. That's it."

Toby had run down the hall past them to check the rest of the doors, so Kate and Matt tried another.

"This one's a lab," Kate said. "There's some machines and a refrigerator, I think. And lots of bottles and jars all around. And there's pictures of bottles of perfume on the wall. Weird. And some more of ladies in makeup."

Kate hopped down, and Matt stood up slowly. "I think that's what they do here," he told Kate. "They make perfume and lipstick and stuff. You know. That's why there's all the pictures on the wall."

Kate looked at Matt blankly. "Then why would they want puppies? In a laboratory where they make *makeup*?"

"Matt," Toby called. "Nothing down here."

"Okay," Matt said. "Come on, we'll try another floor."

"Where's Rusty," Kate wondered. "Wasn't he with you?"

Matt nodded grimly. "Yeah, but I guess he chickened out. When I took off after you, he must have run off or something. Don't worry, he won't tell."

Matt held open the door to the stairs, and Toby and Kate slipped past him.

Halfway down the steps, Toby paused with his ears pointed up as though he were listening. "Come on," he yelped. He raced down the steps with Matt and Kate close behind him. At the door to the second floor he stopped and waited for them. He pawed the door impatiently until Matt opened it.

This door opened onto a hall like the other. But there were fewer doors, which meant the rooms were larger. Even the children, with their inferior human noses, could smell dog and rat and rabbit. Down the hall, so softly that the children had to strain to hear, a dog was whining mournfully.

Matt slipped his hand under Toby's collar. "Here we go, boy," he whispered. "Stay calm."

The children tiptoed into the hall and looked around. "Ready?" Matt asked. He boosted Kate up on his knee in front of the first door. Toby got up on his hind legs to try to see, too.

"Oh!" Kate exclaimed. "Matt, it's rabbits. Hundreds and hundreds of them, all in wire cages stacked one on top of another. They look so cute!"

Kate jumped down and tried the door. It opened easily, and the children slipped inside. "Matt, look," Kate cried. "Look at their *eyes*. Their eyes are all red and sore. Look at that one, his poor eyes are swollen shut."

Toby whined softly and pressed himself against Matt's legs.

"And, Matt, look at this bunny. There's a patch on his side where his skin's all gone, and you can see his ribs sticking out. Oh, the poor thing!"

"Matt," Kate asked suddenly, twisting her hands together, "is this a hospital for sick rabbits?"

Matt hesitated. He wasn't sure what it was, but he knew it wasn't a hospital. "I don't know, Kate," he said at last.

Toby had never chased a wild rabbit, but he'd gone after plenty of squirrels and cats and mice. It was fun, although he'd never quite managed to catch one. Chasing little furry animals made him feel wild and fierce, the way a dog needs to feel sometimes. He'd seen rabbits before, though, be-

97

cause Kate's friend Kelly had a pet lop-ear she'd brought over on Easter Sunday. Toby had thought about chasing that little bunny and hearing it squeal. But he didn't have any desire to chase these poor caged creatures. There was nothing of the wilderness in this bright, foul-smelling room. Toby smelled only fear and medicine and the grassy scent of alfalfa pellets.

"Come on, Kate," Matthew said hurriedly. "We've got to find the pups if they're here." He took Kate's hand and pulled her out of the room. This time she didn't resist him.

"We heard a dog whining before," Matt reminded her quietly. "Let's try to find him. Toby, you check all the doors, starting at the far end of the hall. We'll try up here."

Toby slunk off down the hall, keeping close to the wall. He was happy Matt had caught up with them, but he couldn't help wishing Polly had come along, too. There were times when nothing but another set of sharp teeth could make a dog feel really safe.

More rabbits. Toby snorted in disgust and tried again. Rats this time, he thought. He'd never liked the smell of a rat. He moved to the last door at the end of the long hallway and lowered his nose to the crack at the foot of the door, taking short, sharp breaths.

Puppy. There was an odor of puppy coming from under this door, and a smell of grown dogs, too. Toby gave a sharp, low bark to signal Matt and Kate.

"Puppies," he woofed. "In here! Hurry, Matt!"

Matt and Kate raced down the hall, their sneakers slapping noisily against the hard tile.

Matt boosted Kate up so that she could peek through the glass in the door. "I don't see anybody," she said, hopping down. "Just lots more cages."

Matt opened the door, and they walked cautiously into the roomful of dogs.

"Oh, Matt," Kate breathed. "Oh, no! What's wrong with them all?"

Matt just stood and stared. He'd never seen so many dogs, not even in a pet store. They were one to a cage, in wire enclosures hardly larger than what the rabbits had been kept in. Most of the dogs were smallish, and some of them puppies. They were listless, most of them, staring dull-eyed at the children, hardly even curious about Toby. Some of them had funny wide-brimmed collars around their necks to prevent them from licking or touching their bodies, and lots of them were missing patches of fur in places. There were five stacks of cages up and down, and about twelve across. Matt tried to figure that out in his head, but he kept getting distracted. Anyway, he thought there were fifty cages or so, and only a few were empty.

Fifty dogs, Matt thought, and then it dawned on him what was strangest of all. Except for a whine or a whimper here and there, not one of the dogs was barking or yipping or scratching against the wire of its cage. The room was so quiet that he could hear the regular sniffing that meant Kate was about to burst into tears.

Toby whined and pressed his flanks against the bottom row of cages. One of the dogs, a mixed-breed that looked like it was mostly terrier, got up and pressed his nose against the wire. Toby growled and wagged his tail.

"Yip," the little dog said tentatively. Toby wagged his tail and answered softly. A dog on a higher row, a silver poodle, growled and pawed, trying to get Toby's attention. "Rowf," he said. "Rrow, rrow, rrow, RROW!"

Toby looked up and yelped an answer.

"Woof," called a deep-voiced basset pup on the top row. "Yip, yip, yip!" answered the terrier. "Rrow, rrow, rrow, rrow," insisted the silver poodle. Toby paced back and forth in front of the cages, woofing softly. Matt couldn't tell if he was communicating with the other dogs or if they were all just excited.

"SSSHhh," Matt hushed. "Quiet, everybody. We don't want anybody to—"

"Oh, Matt, LOOK!" Kate said, getting up on tiptoe to reach a cage at the top of the far stack. "It's the cutest thing." Before Matt could stop her, she had unfastened the wire door to the cage and lifted out a fluffy half-grown puppy. He was a lovely soft orange-brown, with a thick ruff of fur around his neck, and tiny jet black eyes. His tail beat furiously against Kate's arm as she held him close to her chest. He looked a little like Toby and a lot like Polly. "Oh," Kate said, "he's a *baby*!"

Toby looked at the puppy in Kate's arms and sniffed deeply. He gave a joyous yip. "Ranger!" he barked, almost knocking Kate down in his enthusiasm.

Most of the dogs were pressed frantically against the front of their cages, now, seeing that Kate had freed the little puppy. Some of the dogs were barking, and some were whining pathetically. Some seemed too sick and weak to make any sound at all. One of these was a medium-size black dog with

101

long legs and thin, bony flanks. This one eyed Matt sadly and let his tail beat weakly against the bottom of his cage. "Kate," Matt whispered, "hang on a minute. Toby, do you see your other pups? What is this place? What's wrong with these dogs?"

"Oh, Matt," Toby began, pressing noses with the thin black dog. His voice was loud, so that Matt could hear him over the din of all the other dogs. "Matt, it's terrible. They—the humans—they come in three times a day and rub awful stuff into the dog's hides, stuff that burns that they can't lick away. Some of them have to swallow nasty-tasting medicine that makes them sick and weak, and . . . and—"

"SSHSHHH!" Matt waved frantically toward the door. The knob was turning. They were about to be caught. Toby scrambled across the room and dived under a desk. Matt tackled Kate and half pushed her, half dragged her into the shadow behind a tall filing cabinet. She held the little pup tight against her chest, and after a moment he stopped struggling and snuggled as close as he could.

The door opened, but Matt and Kate, huddled together with their eyes closed, couldn't see who came in. They heard someone moving around, trying to quiet the dogs. The voice was a young man's.

"Hush, you dogs," he said irritably. "Now what's got you all going? It's not feeding time already."

The dogs began to quiet down and move to the backs of their cages, trying not to be noticed. They all knew this man. He was one of the ones that came and put the stinging stuff on their eyes and in their mouths and noses.

"Hey, now," came the man's gruff voice. "I see what's got you mutts excited. Looks like somebody's made an escape."

Kate and Matt opened their eyes wide and stared at each other. Kate had forgotten to close the wire door after she'd taken Ranger out of his cage.

"Here, poochy, poochy," the man said. "Where are you, poochy?"

Matt peeked around the side of the filing cabinet. The man was down on his hands and knees, checking under the row of cages. If he searched the room, he'd find them.

"Here, boy," the man said, whistling softly. The room was nearly quiet again. "Come out, come out, wherever you are."

Matt reached for Ranger, meaning to put him on the floor where the man could find him. Maybe the man would put Ranger back in his cage and leave. But Kate shook her head fiercely. She pressed the pup against her chest so tightly, it was a wonder he didn't yelp.

Matt gestured frantically, trying to make her let go.

"Okay, fella," the man said. "I'm gonna come looking." The children heard his footsteps move across the room, pausing now and then as he looked around him. "Now, which one is it got away," he wondered aloud. "The basset? Naw, I see him. And it's not the poodle."

The man's footsteps came close to the children. His pale hand touched the edge of the filing cabinet. In a moment he would look behind it and discover them, huddled against the wall. Matt sucked in his breath and tried to feel brave.

"*There* you are!" Matt's stomach flipped over as he waited for the pale hand to grab him and haul him out.

Then the man's hand disappeared, and the children heard his footsteps moving away again. "Okay, mutt. Back in the cage, and this time *stay* there."

A moment later the door opened and closed, and the children crept out into the room. Toby was locked in the cage where Ranger had been before.

He tilted his head in a friendly way and licked Matt's hand as Matt worked with the latch, trying to get the door open. When the door finally opened and Toby came out, Matt could see that the dog was shivering with fear.

As quietly as he could, Matt opened the door onto the long hall. When he was sure no one was around, he led Toby, Kate, and Ranger down the hall and into the stairwell. There, making his voice hardly more than a soft growl, Toby questioned the puppy about other places in the building dogs might be hidden. Ranger was very young, and he couldn't remember things very well yet. Besides that, he was a little afraid of Matt and Toby. He wished he could just curl up inside the little girl's sweatshirt and take a nap. But Toby persisted, and finally the little dog spoke up.

"Yip, yip, yip," he began. Matt and Kate listened carefully, but Toby had to translate.

"He says there's a big room where he stayed when he first came here, a very cold room." Toby explained. "A woman brought him and his brothers and sister and a lot of other dogs. He stayed in that big room for a long time, and then one day a man came and took him to the room where we found him. He's only been there a couple of days, I think, from what he says. But he doesn't know where the first room was. His sense of direction isn't very good yet.''

Kate said, ''He's just a baby.''

''It sounds as though that first place was probably a storage room,'' Matt said thoughtfully. ''Maybe in the basement, since Ranger says it was cold. Anyway, we can start by looking there.''

Ranger yipped again and Toby whined softly and pushed his nose against Matt's leg. ''He says the first day he was here, on this floor, four dogs died,'' Toby said softly. ''And since then, three more. But he thinks they were all grown dogs. So they couldn't have been our puppies.''

Toby gave a deep sigh. ''That silver poodle said he was kidnaped from his own yard,'' he told Matt. ''And those young collies, their owner thought they were going to live on a big ranch in Arizona!''

Matt met Kate's eyes. ''Lucy Simons never took the puppies to any farm,'' he said grimly. The people here are using dogs for experiments. Lucy Simons gets dogs—by stealing them, or by lying to their owners—and sells them to this lab to be used for testing hairspray and hand lotion and stuff.

You know, to see if it'll make a person's eyes burn or skin itch or anything.''

Toby sighed and pressed his head against Matt's knee. Matt patted the dog's head and scratched behind Toby's ears. "Come on, everybody," he whispered. "Let's try and find our way to the basement.''

Chapter Nine

Rusty didn't know what to do. Matt and his dog and his goofy little sister were somewhere upstairs, looking for some litter of puppies, although Rusty didn't half understand why Matt thought the dogs would be here. To tell the truth, Rusty had been having so much fun sneaking around, riding the bus, tricking Matt's mother and his own father, that he hadn't paid much attention to the crazy story about the talking dog and the four missing puppies.

But now this security guard said she was going to have to call the police if Rusty wouldn't tell her his name and address and phone number. And

Rusty knew that however much trouble he'd be in with his dad, it would be double if the police were involved. Then again, the longer he stalled, the more time Matt and Kate would have to do whatever it was they were doing.

"You know you've got to tell sooner or later," the lady said reasonably. "Why not make it now, and save us all a lot of trouble? And then I could get you a nice cold soda to sip while you wait for your mom and dad to come and get you."

Rusty shook his head. "Don't have a mom, and don't want a soda," he said sullenly.

"Then," the woman said, a little edge to her voice this time, "I'm afraid I'll have to call the police."

Rusty shrugged, but he noticed that she didn't reach for the phone.

"Go ahead," he said, as if he couldn't care less. "Be my guest."

The guard frowned. "Why don't you just tell me your name and address, young man? You could save us both a lot of trouble."

Now she looked very irritated, and a little nervous, too. Rusty was beginning to think she didn't want to call the police at all, and not just to save herself some trouble.

"In fact," Rusty said, "I wish you would call

them. I'd love it if you'd call them. I think it's a very good idea for you to call the police right *now*."

The woman got up and clasped her hands behind her back as a white-jacketed man came out from the elevator bank. "Oh, Dr. Phillips," she called. "May I see you a moment, sir?"

The man frowned and sighed irritably, but he walked over to the security desk. "What is it, Miss Johnson? And who is this rascal? Is this our little intruder?"

Rusty curled his lip. This guy was totally sickening.

Miss Johnson nodded. "He refuses to give his name and address, sir. He says I should call the police!"

"Little soldier, eh?" Dr. Phillips gave Rusty an ugly smile.

Rusty was beginning to think these two adults were behaving very strangely indeed. They definitely didn't want to call the police. Could they be trying to hide something that was going on in this building?

"Okay," Rusty said suddenly. "You can call my dad. He's working late tonight, but I know he'll come and get me."

"Good boy," Dr. Phillips said brightly. Miss

Johnson reached for her telephone. "What's his name, son?"

"His name is Jim Eddinger," Rusty replied innocently. "And you can reach him at the *Los Angeles Gazette*. He's a reporter there."

Miss Johnson snatched her hand from the phone as if it had burned her. "Oh, my," she said softly. "A newspaper reporter. Well."

Rusty smiled grimly. He was definitely on to something. These people didn't want the police, and they didn't want any reporters nosing around, either. They were trying to hide something.

"Well, indeed," the doctor echoed heartily. "The *Los Angeles Gazette*. That's all the way downtown, isn't it, son? I'd sure hate for this young fellow's dad to have to come all that way for something so harmless as a rock through a window, eh, Miss Johnson?"

The security officer nodded. "Yes, sir," she agreed.

"Live around here, son?" the man asked Rusty.

"Not too far," Rusty answered.

"Okey-dokey, Miss Johnson. I think this boy's learned his lesson. No need to call his dad and probably earn him a whipping. What say we just show him the door and let him get on home?"

Miss Johnson nodded again, and Rusty stood

up, trying to act scared and grateful. He figured he'd go out the front door and halfway down the block, and wait there for Matt and Kate and Toby. Then they'd all go home together. If Matt's mom and his dad had gotten together and found out they had all sneaked out and lied to cover up, well, they'd all be in trouble. But at least they'd all be safe, Rusty figured.

It was a good plan and it might have worked, too. Except that as Miss Johnson unlocked the door and held it open for Rusty, Dr. Phillips's elevator arrived. The doors opened, and out spilled Matt, Kate, Toby, and what looked to Rusty like half a dozen clumsy, ragged dogs.

"Great day in the morning!" Dr. Phillips shouted.

"Kate, run for it," Matt yelled.

"Save the puppies," Toby barked, and the puppies joined in with him, all of them squealing and yelping and howling just for the fun of it. The poor things had been found curled together in one tiny cage, warm and cozy, not realizing they were in any danger at all.

"You children, halt!" Miss Johnson commanded, but she was too late. Kate had spotted Rusty and taken off straight for him and the open door, with Ranger tucked under her sweatshirt, and another one of Toby's pups under her arm.

A third pup tumbled after Kate. As the doctor reached for them, Toby darted in front of him and bared his teeth savagely. "Touch them," he growled, "and I'll take your arm off."

Dr. Phillips couldn't understand Toby, but he more or less got the message. "Call the handler," he shouted to Miss Johnson, but she'd already thought of that. The young man who'd locked Toby in a cage upstairs came tearing down the hall with a net and a muzzle.

"You stay away from my dog," Matt warned, scooping up the last stray puppy.

While the adults were distracted by Matt, Katie had managed to get out the door with the two she was carrying and one of the others. Rusty hesitated for just a moment. Then he pushed the door shut behind. He grabbed one of Kate's puppies with one hand and then he grabbed her arm. "Come on," he said, hurrying her down the front walk. When they were a safe distance away, he pushed her down behind a bush and set the little pup onto her lap with its brothers.

"Poor babies," Kate cried, trying to cuddle all of them at once. They scrambled over her, licking her face and nuzzling her cheeks and chewing her hair. At first Ranger was overjoyed to see the others. Then he began to seem a little jealous. He poked his head out of Kate's shirt and took a nip at his biggest brother, the fluffy brown-and-white.

"Stay there, Kate," Rusty whispered. "Don't move, hear me?" Then he took off back toward the laboratory.

Rusty had hoped that somehow Matt and Toby would have gotten away with the last puppy so they could all go home. What he saw when he crept up to the solid glass door made him feel sick and scared inside. The creepy-looking doctor had Matt held tight with his arm behind his back. Matt's face was streaked with angry tears. The young man and the security guard held the snapping, snarling Toby down on his back. As Rusty watched, they managed to slip the steel muzzle over the dog's face so he couldn't bark or bite. The bewildered puppy just sat watching, letting her tail thump feebly against the cold floor, as if she hoped it was all a game.

Rusty stayed close to the ground and edged closer to the side of the building so no one would see him. It looked as though the doctor and the guard were arguing about something. Then the elevator doors opened, and a man and a woman hurried out. Rusty couldn't hear what anyone was saying, but he could tell they were disagreeing. Everyone was waving and pointing at Toby and then at Matt.

Rusty hesitated, but not for long. He backed away from the door and down the walk to where he'd left Kate and the puppies hidden in the bushes. He meant to ask Kate for a quarter so that he could find a gas station and call his father. Rusty half expected that Kate would have disobeyed him and tried to get back in the building to help Matt. But no, she was there, kneeling on the grass at the center of a crooked half circle of solemn puppies.

As Rusty watched, Kate and the dogs put their faces up to the dark, star-sprinkled sky and began to howl.

"Kate," Rusty said, nearly shouting to be heard over the awful racket, "what do you think you're doing?"

Kate stopped howling and looked at him. "We're praying," she explained, "to Sirius, the brightest star in the heavens. Toby said Sirius is the guardian of canines, and the keeper of dog magic."

Rusty nodded. "Yeah, sure he did, Kate. Sure he did."

For once Rusty's sarcasm didn't bother Kate a bit. "I don't know if *I* can pray to Sirius or not," she said, "but I'm showing these puppies how to. We're asking for dog magic to save Toby and Wanda and all the other dogs in the laboratory."

"Wanda?"

Kate gestured impatiently. "Toby's last pup," she said. "The one that got caught inside with him." Then, ignoring Rusty, she turned her face back up to the stars and joined the puppies in a long, soulful howl.

Rusty had forgotten to get change from Kate, but he found two dimes in his back pocket. He tried Matt's mother first, but no one answered there, and the phone wouldn't return his money. Finally he called the newspaper collect. The receptionist said his father wasn't answering his phone.

"He *has* to be there," Rusty wailed. "This is an emergency!"

"An emergency?" A receptionist at a newspaper is always interested in emergencies. "Shall I ring the police for you?"

Rusty bit his lip. "Yes," he decided. "I think you'd better." He quickly gave her the name and address of the lab. Almost as soon as he hung up, he heard sirens in the distance.

When Rusty rounded the corner onto Randall Road, he was relieved to see an empty patrol car parked in front of the Bremer building. The police were already there. Everything was going to be all right, he thought. Then a terrible high-pitched shriek sliced through the night. Rusty turned to where he'd left Kate and the puppies praying to the Dog Star.

"Let me go!" Kate screamed. A big policeman had her wrist in one hand and was trying to take something from her with the other. "Let go, let go, LET GO OF ME!"

As Rusty watched in horror, the policeman got whatever it was away from her and handed it to a young man in a blue lab coat. Then Rusty realized that it was the little golden dog she'd been carrying under her shirt.

"Come on, honey," the policeman said gently, tugging on Kate's wrist, as the man in the lab coat dumped the pup into a small wire cage and carried it inside. "Let's go inside and call your mother."

It was a horrible scene, but Rusty almost laughed when Kate kicked the policeman in the shins as hard as she could, and wrenched her hand away from him.

"I want my brother," she shouted. "Where's my BROTHER?"

The policeman grabbed Kate's sleeve and dragged her up the walk and into the lobby. He was not being quite as gentle as he'd been before. Rusty followed as quietly as he could. Oh, why had he let the receptionist call the police? It didn't look as though they were helping at all! And why couldn't his father or Aunt Gretchen have been home?

In the lobby, Matt was sitting still and white-faced in a metal chair. The policeman led Kate to where he was and squatted down, talking to Matt with his back to the doors. The security guard, some of the doctors and lab technicians, and another policeman were in a circle, all talking at once. Toby was stretched out, ominously still, on the floor. All four puppies were huddled in the small cage, watching their father with big, scared brown eyes.

Rusty pushed the door open a crack and whistled softly, trying to get Matt's attention. But at that moment Kate noticed Toby lying on the floor, and she began to scream.

"Toby! *Toby!*" She ran to him and threw her arms around him, struggling to get the metal muzzle off him, but he didn't move. "Matt, what's the matter with Toby?"

"They gave him a shot," Matt said dully. He was trying hard not to cry.

Kate jumped up. "You *killed* him," she yelled,

running straight at a technician with her hands balled into fists.

"Now, hold it!" the man protested, reaching for Kate.

"STOP," one of the policemen said sternly, trying to grab her.

"You get off my sister," Matt shouted. He jumped up and grabbed Kate's hand.

"Matt, Kate! Over here," Rusty called, holding the door open.

"There he is," the security guard hollered. "There's the other one! Get him!"

Matt and Kate raced out the door, and the three children tore off down the walk. But the policemen were too fast for them. One of them grabbed Matt's shirt collar, and the other got his arm around Rusty's chest. Kate scooted off the walk and onto the lawn, dancing away from the security guard, who was trying to catch her.

"DOG MAGIC," she yelled as loud as she could. "Please, Sirius, we need DOG MAGIC, we need it now!" And then, as the adults watched in astonishment, Kate dropped to her knees, threw her head back, and howled.

"Forget the youth authority," Officer Daniels said to Officer Zipkin. "This kid's ready for the loony bin." Then, catching the security guard's stern eye on him, Officer Daniels added, "a psychiatric hospital, I mean."

Officer Zipkin started to answer, but he was interrupted by a screech of tires coming from down the block.

"OWWWWWWOOOOOOH," Kate howled. From within the building everyone could hear a faint answering howl, and then another and another until it seemed as though a thousand dogs were inside clamoring to be free.

"OWWWWWOOOOOH," Kate howled again. No one tried to stop her. There was something moving and frightening, too, about the little girl kneeling in the cool grass leading the unseen dogs in prayer.

"OWWWOOOOOOH," Kate howled, and then a car door slammed and Gretchen Baker shouted, "What are you doing to my *daughter*?"

Kate jumped up and ran to her mother, who had gotten out of a taxi and now stood, her face bright with anger, facing down the doctors and technicians and police.

"Mama," Kate shouted, running across the grass. "Uncle Jim! It worked, it worked. We made DOG MAGIC!"

Mike, the cab driver who had dropped Kate off earlier, stood beside Mrs. Baker, trying to figure out what was going on. He didn't know exactly what had made him go back to the house where he'd picked the little girl up. He'd just had a bad feeling about leaving her alone at this building at night. He'd kept thinking about it as he worked, and finally he'd driven back to the house on Laurel Street. And sure enough, when he'd gotten there, a frantic woman and a bewildered man had been in great need of his cab.

Officer Daniels pulled his notepad out of his hip pocket and approached Mrs. Baker. Uncle Jim had pulled his own notepad out of his pocket and was busily jotting notes. The researchers watched him suspiciously. "Are you the mother of these children?" Officer Daniels asked Mrs. Baker. He looked at Uncle Jim. "And are you the father?"

Mrs. Baker answered. "I'm the mother of two, he's the father of the other," she said, hugging Kate tight. Then she drew Matt and Rusty close to her. "And we'll sort all this out in a minute. But first of all, where is our dog, Toby?"

Suddenly everyone was talking at once. Dr. Phillips was smiling and saying in a smooth, phony voice that everyone might as well just calm down and go home. No harm done, he kept saying, twisting his red-knuckled hands around and around.

Officer Daniels was talking to the security guard, and Officer Zipkin was trying to listen to Matt and Rusty and Mrs. Baker all at once. Uncle Jim was walking around listening to everybody and making notes on his little pad.

No one noticed when Kate slipped her hand into Mike the cab driver's. She pulled him into the brightly lit lobby, where Toby lay still and silent on the cold floor.

"We're baffled," Dr. Phillips was saying outside. "Why would these children break into our lab and try to steal our animals?"

"Toby's *our* dog," Matt said angrily. "And those puppies you were getting ready to experiment on are our puppies, too!"

"*Our* puppies?" Mrs. Baker asked, bewildered.

"*Experiment on?*" Uncle Jim asked. "On dogs? Pretty strict rules and regulations about that kind of stuff, aren't there?"

"Besides, lots of those dogs upstairs *belong* to people," Matt went on. "They're stealing dogs, and tricking people to get them, and—"

"There's no way you could know that," Dr. Phillips snapped. Then he flushed and clapped his hand over his mouth. "What I mean to say is, we conform to every standard. Our subjects are made as comfortable as possible, in roomy cages, with—''

''That's a lie!'' Matt yelled. ''The dogs upstairs aren't comfortable at all. They're stuffed into tiny cages, and the wire bottoms hurt their feet, and they're scared, too. They know what's going to happen to them.''

''Matt,'' Mrs. Baker said quietly.

''Mom,'' Matt pleaded, ''we saw these rabbits with sores all over them, and blind eyes, and dogs in tiny little cages and . . . and—''

Uncle Jim looked up from his notebook. ''We're going to look into this, Matt,'' he said. ''There may be a story in this for the newspaper. And as far as the mistreatment of these animals . . . well, I'll bet these officers can call someone to come out and look around. Isn't that right?''

Officer Daniels nodded. His shin didn't hurt anymore, and he was beginning to like this strange family quite a bit. ''When we moved into our apartment,'' he said slowly, ''my wife let our dog, Zipper, go to a man who answered our ad in the paper. We loved Zipper, but we thought he'd be unhappy without a yard to play in. I'd sure hate to think—''

''So,'' Uncle Jim said, ''why don't you go on with your story, Matt?'' He put his arm around

Rusty's shoulder and gave Matt an encouraging smile.

"Okay," Matt agreed. "So then he grabbed me, and they got Toby down on the floor and put a muzzle on him and stuck him with a big needle, and—"

"They did what to our dog?" Mrs. Baker hollered. She turned and hurried toward the lobby, and everyone followed and crowded in the doors.

Mike had managed to unfasten the muzzle from Toby's face, and now Kate sat cross-legged on the floor with the dog's head on her knee. Big tears rolled down her face and into Toby's golden fur. Mike knelt next to her, trying to organize the four puppies he'd let out of their cage. As everyone watched, the littlest puppy, Ranger, scrambled over his father. He licked Toby's muzzle and his closed eyes.

And then Toby's eyes opened, and he sat up and stretched and yawned and looked around and blinked.

"Toby!" Kate squealed, hugging him.

"Toby!" Matt shouted happily. "Are you okay?"

"Toby," Mrs. Baker called softly.

"Yrow." Toby yawned, stretching again. He

stood up awkwardly and nosed the pups. Then he ambled over to Matt. "Woof," he said happily, licking Matt's hand. "Woof, woof."

And no one, not even the children, could understand a word he said.

Chapter Ten

✜

It was very late when everyone got back to the Bakers' house that night. First they had waited for the Animal Friends Society to come and look around the laboratory, despite Dr. Phillips's angry protests. Some of the dogs had tattoos on their ears, and these were taken away in vans so that their owners could be called.

Uncle Jim said it looked as though the children had discovered a dognaping ring. He didn't know if Dr. Phillips would go to jail or not. But he thought the laboratory would be closed down for the time being. And he decided to go back to his office at the newspaper and begin writing up the story of how the puppies were rescued. He said that once people knew what was happening to animals at Bremer Laboratories, the company would probably go out of business.

Only two of the pups rode home snuggled up against Toby on the backseat of Mike's cab. Ranger wouldn't come out from under Kate's sweatshirt. In the end she had to let him ride there, warm and safe against her bare skin. Hal got to ride curled up next to Mike because Mike had decided to adopt him. Matt and Kate had given their permission, and Toby didn't seem to object.

So Hal was going to be a working dog, riding around with Mike all day, meeting new people and maybe new dog passengers, as well.

Matt and Rusty rode up front with Mike, because Rusty was going to spend the night after all. It would be too late for him to go home when Uncle Jim finished at the newspaper.

"Mommy," Kate asked sleepily, "what's going to happen to Lucy Simons?"

"Well," Mrs. Baker answered, "you gave the police her address, didn't you? And they promised to look into it. There is a law against tricking people, and that's exactly what she did—pretending to adopt a puppy when you really plan to sell it to a laboratory for research."

Kate nodded. "She's a bad person."

Mrs. Baker hesitated. "People do bad things to animals," she said. "And to other people, too. Sometimes it doesn't mean they are bad people, exactly. It just means they haven't thought about what they're doing. Or they have thought about it, but for some reason, well—"

"They want the money," Rusty said cynically.

"Now, Rusty—"

"But Mom," Kate interrupted, tucking her feet under Toby's warm side. "What's going to happen to the puppies? Can we keep them?"

"Well," Mrs. Baker said, pulling Kate's head against her shoulder. "Hal's taken care of. He's got a good home."

As if he'd recognized his name, Hal crawled up over Mike's shoulder and yawned, showing Mrs. Baker and Kate the inside of his pink mouth.

"And Mrs. Brown called tonight," Mrs. Baker went on. "She told me you kids had been there, and what you'd said about those puppies being Toby's children." Matt looked over his shoulder at Kate and gave her a guilty smile.

"You children told some stories tonight, and we'll deal with that later," Mrs. Baker said grimly. Matt and Kate weren't fooled. They might have to

129

do extra chores or be grounded for a week or so, but their mother wasn't really angry with them. Toby's tail thumped weakly against the car seat. He was still groggy from the shot he'd been given at the laboratory.

"Mom," Matt said, "I'm sorry I told you a lie, about Uncle Jim's taking all of us to a dog show. I was too scared to tell you the truth about how I'd lost Kate, and . . ."

"Yes?" Mrs. Baker said dryly. "Do go on, Matt."

Matt flushed.

"Okay," she relented. "I said we'd discuss all that later, and we will. For now, let's just say I was a little suspicious when you called, and even more so after Mrs. Brown called. So I called Uncle Jim, just in case, and—lo and behold—he knew absolutely nothing about any dog show, and he thought I had you children safe with me!"

"Oops," Matt said.

"Yes," Mrs. Baker agreed. "Oops is right. We were frantic. But it was the oddest thing. We could hardly think where you kids might be. Uncle Jim raced right over from his office, and we were just about to drive around the neighborhood looking for you three. Then Mike pulled up in his cab and told me about you, Kate, calling a cab for yourself and taking it all the way to Santa Monica!''

Kate pressed her lips together, trying to look serious and sorry. If she laughed now, she'd really be in trouble.

''So,'' Mrs. Baker went on, ''we were very lucky that Mike was concerned enough about you to investigate, Kate.''

''It wasn't luck,'' Kate replied. ''It was dog magic, sent by Sirius, the Dog Star, the brightest star in the heavens.'' Kate looked at Toby, expecting him to sit up and bark, or at least wag his tail. But he snoozed on, ignoring the human conversation.

''Okay, Kate,'' Mrs. Baker said fondly. ''We're all tired. This has been a big night.''

Matt looked at Kate over the back of the seat and rolled his eyes. Kate stuck her tongue out, fast, so their mother couldn't see.

''Anyway,'' Mrs. Baker continued, ''Mrs. Brown said to tell you kids she couldn't find a number for that Lucy woman who'd supposedly adopted the puppies. She said that if she did come across it, she'd call right away, because she'd decided she wants to keep Wanda for her own.''

Toby wagged his tail again and pressed his nose

into Wanda's fur. She was stretched out beside him, fast asleep.

"So that takes care of Wanda," Rusty said wistfully. "How many puppies are left?"

"Two," Matt said. "Preston and Ranger. Ranger's the little orangy-brown puppy Kate's got under her sweatshirt, and Preston's the one that looks like a black-and-white version of Toby. The other ones we saved will be returned to their owners."

"Preston's a cute one," Rusty said. "He's going to be a big, friendly dog, I can tell."

"Well," Mrs. Baker said, "Preston's already been promised to someone, too, so that just leaves one puppy in need of a home."

"Preston's been promised to someone?" Rusty sounded sad. "Too bad. I was sort of hoping— well, never mind." He turned around and looked at Kate over the cramped seat. "Could you pass him up to me? I'd sort of like to pet him a little, I guess."

Kate picked up Preston carefully and gave him to Rusty. The puppy snuggled against Rusty's neck and went to sleep again.

"Just keep him there with you, Rusty," Mrs. Baker said. "Preston's your dog now. I promised your dad you could have him."

"Wow!" Rusty and Matt looked at each other happily. Even Kate had to admit Rusty wasn't all bad. Nobody who loved puppies could be all bad.

Mike guided the cab around a corner and pulled up in front of the Baker house. "Okay, folks," he said. "Hal and I will say good-bye and good-night."

Everybody piled out of the taxi except Kate. She gave Ranger to her mother to hold, and then she leaned over the front seat and put her arms around Mike's neck and kissed him and Hal at the same time.

"Mike," she whispered in his ear, "Toby really did talk, okay? It was dog magic, and I think it's over now, 'cause we don't need it anymore. But he *did* talk. He really, really, *really*, did."

"I believe you," Mike said gently. "Because I *heard* him speak, remember?" And then Mrs. Baker reached into the cab and pulled Kate out, and everybody stood on the sidewalk and waved until the cab was out of sight.

"We'll take Wanda down to the Browns' house tomorrow morning," Mrs. Baker said, unlocking the front door. "Right now, I think we could all use a glass of milk and then bed. Matt, you and Rusty fix a place for the puppies to sleep in the

kitchen with Toby, and then get into your paja-
mas.''

''Mom,'' Matt said, ''can I tell her now? Can I
tell her?''

''*May* I tell her,'' Mrs. Baker corrected.

''Tell me *what*?'' Kate demanded.

''Oh, kids,'' Mrs. Baker said innocently, ''I think
it can wait till morning.''

''Tell me WHAT?'' Kate said again, squeezing
Ranger so hard, he squeaked.

''May I, Mom? May I tell her?''

Mrs. Baker smiled at Matt. ''Oh, well, I guess
so. Why not?''

''Tell me!'' Kate yelled. ''Tell me, tell me, TELL
ME!''

''Ranger's *yours*!'' Matt said. ''We're gonna keep
him!''

''Rrow, rrow, rrow,'' Toby barked enthusiastically. Matt felt a little bit sad. Toby couldn't talk
anymore—or at least the children couldn't understand him. He knew the dog magic was over. But
then he looked around him, at his mother and his
cousin and his sister and the kitchen full of puppies, and he wasn't sad anymore. Not one little
bit.

And in spite of everything Mrs. Baker said, no
one in that house got to sleep that night until

long after midnight. Everyone was too busy
feeding puppies and cuddling puppies and finding out what three happy puppies can do to a
nice neat house when they really set their minds
to it.

ABOUT THE AUTHOR

ANNA COATES lives in Los Angeles with her husband, Frederick, and their dachshund, Baron, who does not speak. *Dog Magic* is her first book for children. She is working on another.

Wild and crazy adventures from
<u>Stephen Manes!</u>